Worth the Wait

by Holy Spirit &
Prophetess Yolanda Perry

But they that wait upon the LORD shall renew their strength;
they shall mount up with wings as eagles;
they shall run, and not be weary; and they shall walk, and not faint.
ISAIAH 40:31

Unless otherwise indicated, Scripture quotations are taken from the King James Version of the Bible.

All brackets represent insertions or paraphrases made by the author.

Worth the Wait
ISBN 0-88144-266-6

P.O. Box 4523
Spanaway, Washington 98387

Contents

Dedication

I dedicate this work to Holy Spirit because You whispered
each and every word into my spirit.
Whenever You found me "at ease in Zion,"
You nudged me ever so gently
to remind me that I needed to hurry up and get this done,
and just look at the finished product.
We Did It!

To my wonderful husband, Keith
And my three awesome children:
Darius the Great, Lady Kadazia & Lady Kyra

To my Dad, Benjamin Allen, Jr & my Mom, Shirley Allen,
It all started with the two of you.

Acknowledgements

Keith Eric Perry, the love of my life (next to Jesus), thank you for allowing me to write this book and telling much of our story. Thank you for your nudge every time I started slacking when you asked, from time to time, "How's your book going?" That reminded me that we are in this together, and I am glad that, together, we have something that is going to make a difference in the Body of Christ and the world as a whole. I am so blessed that you have proven to me that it was well "Worth the Wait!" I love you my Mighty Man of Valor!

My Children, you each inspired me in your own unique and special way. Darius Javar Perry, your words, "I don't want you to go back to work right now because your book is getting ready to take off, and you are going to be traveling all over. I want you to be home as much as you can right now." Kadazia KeSahn Perry "Future Talk Show Host," despite all of your health issues, your priceless personality and ambition to be famous has pushed me to write this "best seller" so that you can share the spotlight with me (Smile). Kyra Elise Perry, the proof of my strength, I will never forget the words you said to me (at the age of 7) in Spanaway Park, "Like TD Jakes in *Mama Made the Difference,* you're going to make a difference soon." How blessed I am that I can call you each my own.

Machelle Wall, Co-Pastor and First Lady of Living His Word Evangelistic Ministries, I am so grateful to you for always being willing to listen and always having just the right words to encourage me when I was going through. I can never repay you for the times you stayed on the phone with me all night long, refusing to say good-bye until I felt a little bit better. It was your question you asked me over and over, "Are you writing this stuff down, because there is a book in all of this?" that encouraged me to attempt this feat. More than any thing, thank you for never ever telling a soul; your level of confidentiality is admirable. I have learned so much from you.

My midwives, Anjanette Hudson-Garner, LaKeith Garner, Kelly Jenkins, Patricia Lemons, Cynthia Pegues, Tammie Sullivan, and Rose Marie Waverly, your encouraging words caused me to "Keep Pushing!" Thank you, to each of you for reading in the embryo stage as I wrote. Jamicka Jones, your anticipation of the next chapter again and again gave me so much confidence in what I was producing. Also, thank you for being genuinely happy for me. An experienced agent could never take your place. Mary Rodriguez, my 69 year old best friend, your attention to detail came through in the end as you read through the book (twice) in one setting.

I wish I could list everyone by name, but to all who believed in me, thank you.

Foreword

Have you ever experienced something so horrendous, so seemingly insurmountable that you were not completely confident that God was going to be able to bring you out of it? Have you ever evaluated the circumstances that were staring you in the face, and wondered to yourself whether or not you were going to be able to withstand them? Have you ever looked to the people in your life who have always been your strength and found that they were helplessly void of any words of comfort or relief? Then perhaps you can relate to the utter perplexity that the author of this book is about to allow you to experience with her.

You see, at the most desperate and desolate times of our lives, the Savior comes and stands with us. He gently reminds us that when He stands with us, He is more than the whole world against us. He encourages us with the words from Joshua 1:5, *I will never leave you nor forsake you.* He lifts us and gives us the strength and courage that we need to keep moving forward when our flesh wants to completely crumble under pressure. Father God lets us know that although we may be completely exhausted from waiting on Him, we are to simply keep waiting. He wants us to be confident in knowing that the only way we can mount up with wings as eagles (See Isaiah 40:31), is by patiently and faithfully waiting on Him.

As I walked through the experiences that Yolanda is about to share with you in this book, one thing became immediately apparent to me. She positively refused to believe that waiting on God was not the absolute right thing to do. Through all the sleepless nights and all the tears, she consistently came back to the words, "but I have to wait on God."

This is not the fairy–tale story that has a beautiful resolution in just a few days. On the contrary, this is a gut–wrenching story that went on for months and into years. But through it all, she continued to wait. She stubbornly believed that the God who had spoken to her heart, to valiantly wait on him, was going to give her the courage and stamina to stand unwaveringly until He brought her prayers to fruition.

Now perhaps you were drawn to this book because you are waiting as well. Maybe, like my daughter in the Gospel, you are waiting for a change to occur in the life of your spouse. Perhaps your wait is concerning your ministry. Possibly, you are faced with financial or emotional issues that you are waiting for God to bring to a conclusion. No matter what circumstances you are faced with or how long you have been waiting to see the hand of God move in your situation, may every page of this woman's experience encourage you to continue to wait. May the words that she has been inspired by the Holy Spirit, to include within these pages, give you the tenacity to look to the hills from whence cometh your help. May the God of Provision, who encouraged her daily, speak to your heart and convince you, the way that He convinced her, that He is more than *Worth the Wait*.

Co–Pastor Machelle Wall

Introduction

But they that wait upon the LORD shall renew their strength; they shall mount up with wings as eagles; they shall run, and not be weary; and they shall walk, and not faint.

Isaiah 40:31

Wait! Before you begin to read these pages, make a commitment this very moment to read this work in its entirety. If the title, *Worth the Wait* peaked your curiosity, the contents within will go further offering you words of comfort, encouragement, and hope as you are in waiting for something from our Heavenly Father right now. Though the illustrations throughout focus primarily on my personal testimonies—the trauma that I personally experienced at particular times in my marriage, my military career, and motherhood—the message is universal to every individual who endeavors to "wait" on God for whatever it is you desire for Him to do in your life. My story serves as a testimony of the awesomeness of God and what He is able to do when we wait on Him and allow Him to move for us, how and when He deems necessary to do so. Simply put, if you are married and need Him to bring peace and reconciliation in your home, then this book is for you. If you are not married, and you want a husband (wife), need a husband (wife), or just gotta have a husband (wife) "right now!", then this book is for you. If God has given you a vision revealing how He wants to use you, and you are frustrated waiting for it to come to pass, then this book is for you. This is not a "how to wait" on God manual strictly for Christians, as I will share how God was at work in my life and the union with my husband well before I ever welcomed Christ into my heart. So for the one holding this book right now and does not know the Lord, but you have been in waiting for something or Someone meaningful to come into your life, this book is for you, too. In short, waiting comes in many forms; but regardless of the circumstance that revolves around your call to a holding pattern, this book was written especially for you.

This manuscript will unveil how my Father, my Comforter, my very Best Friend helped me to endure one of the most difficult trials that I have ever had to go through in my life as He taught me how to await the manifestation of my answers to prayer. In these pages, you will discover how you, too, can master the art of waiting which will result in your experiencing the fullness of what God has in store for you. Though you may have been fixated on your target, the thing that you have been waiting and believing God for, you are going to experience an abrupt shift in your focus upon completion of this book. No more will that which you are waiting for be your driving force, but rather the One who is responsible to bring it into fruition.

When God becomes more important than what we want from Him, it is then that He is willing to respond to our requests, move for us, and reveal to us His desire for our lives. Until our "yes" to His will moves beyond the surface of our lips, and becomes convincing to Him and to ourselves as well, we will remain in a state of dissatisfaction, waiting for what He longs to entrust to us: His promise, His plan, and His purpose for our lives. God's actual place in our hearts is divulged through our obedience to Him as we wait and our willingness to wholly yield ourselves to Him. Once we reach the point of total submission to the Father, He can trust us to fully appreciate what He has in store for us and fathom what He has for us to do. Thus, sometimes our world is shaken, things do not happen how we expect them to or when we want them to in order for God to get our attention and expose to us the true state of our own hearts: Are we really after Him? Or are we after what we can get from Him and/or through Him?

As I began my journey with the Lord endeavoring to wait out an agonizing affliction that I was to undergo in my marriage, I was not prepared for what I ultimately discovered about myself. Before this trial, I thought my love for the Lord was pure and unadulterated. I sang the song, "I love you Jesus...more than anything." Surely I was rooted, grounded, and could not be shaken. Hey, my feet were like hinds' feet and my face like a flint. Nothing could separate me from the love of God, and nothing meant more to me than my relationship with Him, "So I thought!" Be honest with yourself when you answer the question: Does any of this sound familiar to you? My greatest discovery, which was birthed out of an amazingly distressing experience in my marriage, was that my relationship with God was not what I perceived it to be. When I thought that my husband was the focal point of the trial, the Lord hurriedly helped me to realize that, at the time, His focus was not so much on my husband, but rather He was focusing on what He needed to perfect in *me*. What a rude awakening for someone who knew she had it all together. As you read, while yet in waiting, permit God to disclose what it is He wants to perfect in you without limits or boundaries. Allow him to shift your focus from what you believe He needs to do in your situation, and give Him free course to do what He, the Omniscient (All–knowing) One sees fit to do in you. Let Him minister to your needs in a way that only He can trusting that He is aware of what you want, but more importantly, He knows best what you need.

My transparency in this book will certainly leave me vulnerable to much scrutiny, judgment, and criticism. Nonetheless, I am aware that one has to attain a certain level of maturity in God to understand the necessity of letting it all hang out if we are to be effective at reaching those who are lost without directions. Another lesson I learned while on this journey of waiting with the Lord is that it is not my story to hold captive, but rather it is the Lord's to be shared with those who need encouragement as they are waiting on Heaven to move on their behalves. Further, I am not embarrassed or ashamed of any part of what I lived through. It is who I am. It is my testimony of what God has done in my life, my marriage, and in my ministry. I am a living testimony (See 2 Corinthians 3:2 *Ye are our epistle written in our hearts, known and read of all men*). I am in awe that God not only could keep me in the midst of my tribulations, but He could in the end bring me out of them, giving me the ability to tell this story for His purpose, His honor, and His glory. Having been brought through, I recognize and acknowledge that, as a woman of God I now have a responsibility to reach back and help somebody else through. That somebody is you. And this book is my hand reaching back, and I am saying to you this day, "Here my Sister, here my Brother, Here my friend. Take my hand, let me help you through."

The primary illustration that I speak of chronicles the events of the early stages of my marriage as well as a two year separation from my husband, of which Satan used drugs each time as an attempt to destroy his life, his ministry, and claim his soul. I will explain how God kept me *completely* during his departure from our home. The testimonies throughout will give you a glimpse of the goodness and faithfulness of God, and how learning to wait on Him in the most perplexing moments can prove to result in a sort of joy that goes beyond your comprehension. Know that His word is true when He tells us if we wait, He will strengthen us, and in the most difficult times He will make us to soar like eagles, causing others around us to wonder about this God that we serve. You will discover as you read, that regardless of how overwhelming your situation becomes, waiting patiently on the Master will obstruct weariness as it attempts to overtake you. You will realize the benefits of keeping your eyes fixed on Him and the promises that He has already made to you in His Word rather than dwell on your present state. Come let me show you how I waited and the blessings that I received as a result of doing so. Allow me to show you how your decision to keep waiting "until God moves" will bring about the same measure of blessings for you, too.

> *Then Peter opened his mouth, and said, Of a truth I perceive that God is no respecter of persons.*
>
> ACTS 10:34

I say to you one. I say to you all. The same God who did it for me will do it for you, if you will just stand on His Word which says:

> *So shall my word be that goeth forth out of my mouth: it shall not return unto me void [without fruit], but it shall accomplish that which I please, and it shall prosper in the thing whereto I sent it.*
>
> ISAIAH 55:11

So I say to you, Wait! Wait! Wait! Some of you may be asking this question internally: Why? My response to you is: Because, I promise you if it is from God, it is worth it!

Part 1

Setting the Stage

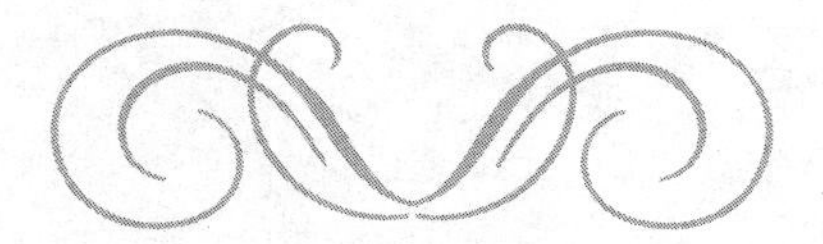

To lay the foundation for this assignment in its entirety, it is necessary to set the stage in the beginning. Setting the stage will help all to understand that there is a process that one must go through to prepare oneself to experience the fullness of what God has promised to him or her. Thus, chapter one begins with a discussion about divine connections, highlighting the benefits of being divinely connected to God, the Father. Chapter two causes one to do some soul searching and thus, affords the opportunity to consider the state of one's relationship with Father God. Finally, chapter three covers the importance of relationship and proper communication with God which, in effect, determines how one communicates with others. Each chapter attempts to help the reader not only prepare for what is to come in the furtherance of this manuscript, but also for the release of whatever he or she is waiting with great expectations for from the Master.

> *Wait on the LORD: be of good courage, and he shall strengthen thine heart: wait, I say, on the LORD.*
>
> PSALM 27:14

Part 1 was written to encourage you that God has and holds, in His hands, everything concerning you. The only thing you must do to receive what He has for you is ensure that you are in right relationship with Him. When you commune with God, as you

should often, all that you desire is there for the taking. When one wholeheartedly commits to God, He seeks out ways to pour out of His goodness for that individual. He does not hesitate to discharge the great things that He holds in store for the one who is willing to totally yield to Him. Once one connects and commits to Him, creates a sure foundation in Him, and opens up the lines of communication with Him, that individual has guaranteed a position of limitless blessings from the bosom of God. Could that one be you? Are you willing to do the necessary ground work to claim the promises of God that are waiting for you? I thought so. Just read with an open heart, and be prepared to make the necessary adjustments in your walk that would position you to receive of His, the Father's, goodness.

Chapter 1

A Divine Connection

I am the vine, ye are the branches: He that abideth in me, and I in him, the same bringeth forth much fruit: for without me ye can do nothing.

John 15:5

Prior to separation, there had to have been a time of coming together, and thus I find it necessary to begin this book with the accounts of how my husband, Keith, and I first met and what ultimately made me consider this man to be the promise worth waiting for. Though you may find the story of how we came together a pleasurable one to read, I must admit that my greatest encounter ever was not when I met my husband, but rather when I hooked up with my Lord and Savior, Jesus Christ. Therefore, this book would be far from complete if I were to eliminate the details of how I met the Master Himself. Had I not known the Lord as I did when our marriage began to take a downward spiral, I do not know that I would have recognized that Keith and I have *A Divine Connection* and that our destinies are intertwined. You see, when we married we became one, and together we are the branches that are attached to the Vine, destined to bring forth much fruit in our ministry of marriage. Somehow God was able to convince me of that as I waited for Him to manifest Himself in our lives. Though I was not serving God when I first met Keith, the Lord already knew us both. More importantly, the Omniscient (All–knowing) One knew the plan and purpose that He has for our life.

> *Before I formed thee in the belly I knew thee; and before thou camest forth out of the womb I sanctified thee...*
>
> JEREMIAH 1:5A

It Was "Like Like" at First Sight

We were both seniors in high school, and Keith had come from New York to live with his grandmother in South Carolina where I resided. Though we were at the same school, it was not there that "he first took notice of me." Hey, this is my story, and I can tell it as I remember it! We officially met at our after school job. I had been working at McDonalds for quite some time, and I was used to the daily routines of a cashier. One day, unexpectedly, there was an interesting turn of events that made being a cashier a bit more fascinating. Now when I reached for the Big Macs and Quarter Pounders with Cheese, I had someone singing to me from the grill.

Yep! That was my Keith. Needless to say, I was elated and no longer dreaded coming in to work. In fact, I was willing to take on a few extra hours here and there.

Grill songs led to a very serious relationship. Well, serious for high school that is. Keith began to drive me home from work, which was usually a very quiet ride since I was extremely shy. But hey, who says you have to verbally communicate in order to have a good relationship? There is more to a relationship than talking, right? I had the privilege of wearing "his" jacket exclusively for about two whole months which at the time made me feel as though I was his queen, wearing a crown. There is no memory of us officially breaking up, as I do not remember ever being directly told that we were no more. Now looking back, there is also no recollection of me ever being told that we were; we just knew it. However, the end, as we knew it then was quite evident when I saw someone else wearing "the jacket" (my crown) that I wore up until the day before. I smile now as I recall the devastation that I felt at seventeen years of age. As I stated before, we were serious.

Even as a teenager, there was something different regarding the way I felt about Keith versus other boys. Most of the boys who pursued me were okay, but there was something that made me fonder of this particular boy. Perhaps it was because he was from out of town, wore the neatest outfits, or had the best haircut. Who knows? I just remember that he had a special place in my heart that I had never allowed anyone else to invade. It is not that I did not like the others but

Keith, I "liked, liked" him. To interpret, I will say, I really liked him (Just one notch below love which at age seventeen I did not yet understand anyway). After our break up, when I was able to recover and regroup, I began to strategize. I was determined to remain connected with him in some way. If that meant being his friend in the midst of humiliation as he dated another girl, then so be it. Through friendship, my hopes were that I could somehow prove to him that I was the one for him. This was no easy feat since I did not talk very much. Perhaps it was my love letters that was responsible for the end result of him finally realizing that he and I were meant to be. Before salvation I might have held to that, but now I have come to the realization that it was God who foreknew the fate of our union. It is our Heavenly Father who knows our present. Moreover, it is the All-Knowing One who created and holds the blueprint for our future.

> *For I know the thoughts [plans] that I think toward you, saith the Lord, thoughts [plans] of peace, and not of evil, to give you an expected end.*
>
> JEREMIAH 29:16

Reunited... With the Trash Collector

God kept me even through my little woes in life despite the fact that I had not yet committed my life to Him. Somehow Keith and I did remain friends over the years and across the miles, as he had eventually relocated back to New York some time after we graduated from high school. Not long after graduating, while preparing to enlist into the U.S. Army, I learned that I was with child. At the time I was devastated over another recent failed relationship, and the military was to be my escape, my new start. It still had not hit me that the Cross is the only place where one can run to for absolute peace, comfort, and refuge.

> *Come unto me all ye that labour and are heavy laden, and I will give you rest. Take my yoke, and learn of me; for I am meek and lowly in heart: and ye shall find rest for your souls. For my yoke is easy, and my burden is light.*
>
> MATTHEW 11:28–30

I remember withholding the information about my pregnancy from my parents for several weeks. Though I knew that my actions could result in the condition that I found myself in, I went into denial. I requested that the doctors do further tests, and they agreed. However, I had to wait for the results to be mailed to me. It seemed like an eternity. My body quickly began to change and was threatening to tell the story on its own.

Despite the fact that I was with child, Keith and I began a long distance relationship across the miles. When I gave birth to my son, Keith came to visit. I bottled up the memory of how gentle he was with Darius. You see, the way to the heart of a mother is through her child. Even though his visit with us was very brief, his actions spoke volumes about his character leaving me with mental notes to refer back to in the years that would follow. I will not share all of the intimate details of how we came back together again. I will, however, tell you that by the time we reunited, I was the mother of two but not yet the wife of one. Nevertheless, Keith, in the innocent immaturity of his youth took a chance on something that was foreign to him (a ready–made family). I was a single parent in the military by this time, and I was struggling to take care of two children without any type of support. It was at this time in my life that God was about to give me another glimpse into the heart of this man, the man whom God would later reveal to me as His Mighty Man of Valor.

When Keith moved to Georgia where I was living at the time, he did not have it all together, if you know what I mean. Conversely, I did not have it all together myself as you have read thus far. He had recently been released from an extended drug rehabilitation program. I had suspicions that He had not successfully completed it, but he never mentioned it, and I never asked. It did not matter to me either way. I always enjoyed our telephone conversations, but I was yearning for an up close and personal companionship, and quite frankly, raising two children alone was becoming intolerable for me. I am reminded of the one time that I called, making preparation for Keith to come and be with us (my children and me), and his mother answered the phone. She asked me not to put him out on the streets, and she made me promise that I would help him get home if things did not work out between the two of us. I assured her that all would be well with us, and I expected us to get along just fine. I never thought for a moment about what his mother was saying to me, and it never dawned on me that Mom might know just a little bit about what it would be like to live with this man. I did not learn exactly what she was hinting at until a few months had passed. To this day, I believe that God strategically hid his flaws and imperfections from me so that I would not miss it when he showed me the true contents of Keith's heart.

It was a Friday night when he de–boarded the Amtrak train, and we headed for Georgia. Though I was proud of the home that I was fortunate enough to put together for my children and me, it was not exactly what one would perceive to be the land flowing with milk and honey. Things were so tight, that I do not even think I had "milk or honey" in my refrigerator at the time. At first light, Monday morning, I allowed him to drive me to work and keep the car so that he could go out job searching. He was hired on the spot. His first job offer was picking up trash in a trailer park which he humbly accepted. Though I knew Keith wanted better, not one day that week did he utter a complaint or grumble about the job or what it paid (which was next to nothing). He worked on the job until that Friday, and he received his paycheck. It was at this moment I declared that he is a keeper. When he picked me up from work, he did not stop by the bank to cash his check, and he did not drive us straight home. He drove us to the local Piggly Wiggly grocery store. When we got to the check out counter (with a basket filled with groceries), he meekly signed over his $81 check that he worked all week to earn, collecting trash.

At that moment I knew that in one week, I had found my soul mate, the one who was just as concerned about the well–being of our family as I was. Even as a sinner, God was able to convince me that beyond his shortcomings, Keith not only has a heart of gold, he also has great purpose and infinite potential. Even before salvation, God kept me in waiting for Keith whom I would share a lifetime of blessings with. Within one month, Keith and I were engaged, and one year later we were married on the anniversary of our engagement resulting in *A Divine Connection,* orchestrated by the Master Himself. Now I must inform you that I am not saying it was God's plan for us to live together before marriage, as that is not scriptural. My decisions were those made when I was not living and walking in the will of the Lord. Hence, the enemy's plan to keep us in bondage to the sin of fornication backfired, as what he intended for evil, God has made it good. Caution: Do not think that if you are living in this situation or are endeavoring to do so, that God will automatically bless your union. Now that you have been enlightened about this wrongdoing, you are accountable to God for the knowledge that you have gained.

> *Therefore to him that knoweth to do good, and doeth it not, to him it is sin.*
>
> JAMES 4:17

Cupid Strikes Again

I was born into a Christian home, to Christian parents, with a dad who was a pastor, but I had never personally met our Heavenly Father. I knew church, but I never knew Jesus Christ as my Lord and Savior. During my youth, I made a conscious choice to not serve the

Lord. It was my belief that God would wait on me until I got good and ready. My reason for not inviting the Lord into my heart had to do with what I saw of young people joining the church: They would do church for a little while, and then they would back away, and the cycle would repeat itself over and over again. I was one that once I made a decision, I stood firm on it without wavering. I vowed that I would uphold this standard when I made my decision to surrender my life to the Lord. As a teenager, I often wrote poems about what it would be like when I committed my life to Christ. In one of my poems I wrote, "There would be no looking back or turning around." To this day, I can say that I never did look back, not even once. That is not to say that I never got weary on my journey with the Lord, but rather when I did, weariness never caused me to consider not serving Him.

In November, 1997 I had a divine encounter which ultimately led to *A Divine Connection* with the Holy One of Israel. When I had returned from a one year tour in Korea, I was required to attend a military school en route to my next duty station. Upon my arrival at the school, I began to feel depressed as I had to be separated from my family once again. When I had reached my lowest point, the Father came and introduced Himself to me in a way that has impacted my life forever. He presented Himself through one of His children, my beloved sister Anjanette (Anjie), with whom I am still "divinely connected" to this very day. The Bible makes it clear what we are to do as Christians in the following passage of Scripture and what results it will bring as well:

Let your light so shine before men, that they may see your good works, and glorify your Father which is in heaven.

MATTHEW 5:16

Until I met this angel sent from Heaven, I had never met a Christian with the joy and peace that radiated from Anjie. I was apprehensive at first, thinking "No one could be this happy for real all the time." Then I realized that "No one could fake being this happy all the time." Thus, I quickly concluded that what she was experiencing was real, and I wanted to experience it for myself. I realized that she knew something and Someone I had not yet come in contact with. I wanted to become familiar and connected with the One who was responsible for the glory that was evident in her life.

There was yet another angel that God already had in place at the school prior to Anjie and me arriving. This angel is named Martha, and she was already attending a local church during the time she was in school. Martha was the conduit that God had in ready position to usher me into my destiny with Him. She invited us both to the church she was attending. At the end of the service, the Pastor asked if he could pray with us individually. My futile attempt to get him off of my case did not work as I said, "I'm no stranger to Christ; my father is a Bishop." That Pastor did not back down; he boldly let me know that I needed a relationship with God for myself. I was appalled. Up until this time, my "daddy–the–bishop" shield had always protected me from anyone trying to witness to me. When I left out of the service that night, I was ready to commit my life to Christ. I cried all night long thinking about it. I had not made the actual commitment to Christ by that time, but it was exciting just getting prepared to do so. The only reason I had not done it yet was that I wanted to give Keith the opportunity to take that step with me. I went home for an extended weekend with my family and hoped that Keith would be ready to receive the Lord with me. He was not at that time, so as I drove from Georgia to Virginia, headed back to school, I surrendered my life to the Lord while driving down the interstate. I literally felt the weights of life and the chains of bondage lift and fall off of me.

When I went back home for the holidays, I was excited and filled with such joy. My husband immediately noticed the difference in me. I had become the Anjie that I had told him about at school (smiling all the time, laughing when there appeared to be nothing funny at all). He became so concerned about my behavior that he even called my mother and told her something strange was going on with me and to find out if she knew whether something was wrong with me. It was bizarre to him at the time, seeing me full of joy all the time. Because he had not accepted Christ yet, he did not have a concept of that experience. Imagine that, another *Divine Connection*. How blessed I am. With the latter connection, I have come to learn that there is nothing I cannot survive. Not even a failed marriage had the ability to break me as long as I was hooked up with the All–Powerful One. Now that is enough to get excited about! I learned through my relationship with Father God that my marriage could stand the tests of the times as long I held onto Him, my Rock. It is comforting to know that my grip of the Rock is secure. You, too, must know that you have a firm grip, so that when life throws curve balls your way (as it did me), your circumstances will not be able to overtake you. You have to know how to get a hold of the Prayer–Answering God in your times of distress as Joab did:

> *And Joab fled unto the tabernacle of the LORD, and caught hold on the horns of the altar.*
>
> 1 KINGS 2:28

When things in your life do not go according to [your] plans, you must yield yourself, shift, and get into a position that will enable you to hear and trust the plan of Almighty God.

Find a Place to Get a Good Grip

When it seems as though life has taken an unsuspected turn, you just have to find your place in it, find a place to get a good grip, and hold on with all your might to the One who has promised that He will never leave you or forsake you. You have to believe and trust that He will never let you fall. The Word from the Everlasting Father to you this day is:

> *...and be content with such things as ye have: for he hath said, I will never leave thee, nor forsake thee.*
>
> HEBREWS 13:5

You may feel like you cannot hold on any longer, like you would break if you were to suffer one more blow. I implore you to dismiss those thoughts of defeat and embrace the promises of God. I entreat you to boldly declare and decree the Word of the Lord which says:

> *Thou hast also given me the shield of thy salvation: and thy right hand hath holden me up, and thy gentleness hath made me great. Thou hast enlarged my steps under me, that my feet did not [and never will] slip.*
>
> PSALM 18:35–36

You may be thinking, "What can you tell me? You don't even understand what I am going through. You can't possibly understand how unbearable it is to wait on God and not hear Him speak a word about your situation for days, weeks, months. You don't know how it feels to be empty and feel as though God is not really there, like He is not really hearing your prayers. You can't possibly understand how it feels when it seems as though your situation is hopeless, so you just decided to get used to it and accept it." The first thing I would say to you, "Vessel in Waiting," is that I understand ever so clearly every one of your distressing thoughts. Further, I say to you, "Don't you dare give up! Don't you dare throw in the towel just yet!" The Omnipotent (All–Powerful) God is clearing His throat and He has a Word for you this day. He is going to minister to you in a way that you have never experienced as you read each page of this manuscript.

Just in case you may be wondering, "What could she say that would encourage me as I wait on God to move for me?" Well, all I can say to that is, I am well–qualified to tell you that whatever you have been believing God for, whatever vision He has shown you, whatever Word He has whispered into your spirit, it is *Worth the Wait.* I speak of my qualifications in confidence and not boast. I have been tried and proven, and as a result He has given me a mandate to write this book just for you. Bishop TD Jakes once preached a powerful message entitled "Prove It." So I will not offer a list of my credentials to you. Rather, I will let you discover them for yourself as you see how the Most High God honored my wait by answering all of my prayers, proving that He heard me all the time, even when I thought He was not listening nearby. Since God is not a respecter of persons, I trust and believe that my writing this book was not to provide mere entertainment but rather to sow a seed of faith into the lives of those who will receive it and believe that if you:

> *Confess your faults...and pray...that ye may be healed. The effectual fervent prayer of a righteous man [or woman] availeth much.*
>
> JAMES 5:16

With that, I conclude this chapter by saying that your summons to reading this manuscript is a divine appointment for you. Further, when you were prompted to read this book, yet another *Divine Connection* took place. Thus, I urge you to allow God to do all that He intends to do in and through you as you complete this journey that you have begun with me.

Chapter 2

Foundational Salvation

For God so loved the world, that he gave his only begotten Son, that whosoever believeth in Him should not perish, but have everlasting life.

John 3:16

That if thou shalt confess with thy mouth the Lord Jesus, and shalt believe in thine heart that God hath raised him from the dead, thou shalt be saved.

Romans 10:9

Scripture tells us that in order to be saved, to walk in oneness with the Lord as our personal Savior, we have to believe in our hearts that God raised Jesus, His only begotten Son, from the dead. Beyond that, we must also make an oral confession of our belief that Jesus is Lord. The key point to note in each of the aforementioned passages of Scripture is that we must *believe.* That means when we enter into salvation, we step into it as faith-filled individuals. It makes me wonder, *What happens to our faith along the way?* If we can believe and have faith about Someone whom we cannot see in order to receive salvation, then why is it that we have trouble believing the same Lord for whatever else we need Him to do in our lives? Rather than decrease in faith, we ought to increase after having walked in oneness with the Lord for 2 months, 2 years, 20 years, and so on. If your faith does not increase, it is an indication that your relationship with God is probably not intact, and that your foundation in salvation is not sure.

> *And the apostles said unto the Lord, Increase our faith.*
>
> LUKE 17:5

There is a direct correlation between your faith level and your level of communication with your heavenly Father. Though, in the subsequent verse, Jesus pointed out to the apostles that they did not need greater faith for what was required of them (See Luke 17:6 *And the Lord said, If ye had faith as a grain of mustard seed...*), the apostles knew that more faith could only be acquired by walking closely with Christ. Likewise, we must acknowledge that in order to get what it is we desire from the Lord, we must be in covenant relationship with Him.

> **Covenant**—stems from the Greek word **diathïkï**, meaning: a contract; a testament

God expects nothing less than total commitment from us—to demonstrate our faith in Him by totally surrendering all that

concerns us to Him. We must also live in total submission to our heavenly Father understanding that without Him, we can do nothing, and we can have nothing. Simply put, without God we are nothing. Acknowledging this fact is a key to unlocking the door to the heart of God, rendering Him compassionately willing to pour out of the goodness of His bosom upon us, granting us the desires of our hearts as according to His will.

> *For in him we live, and move, and have our being...*
>
> ACTS 17:28A

As we walk in the ways of the Lord, He will firmly and strategically place every one of our footsteps. He will make the crooked places straight before us and light our pathways. The Lord promises that He will direct our paths if we would trust Him with our whole heart. Further, He welcomes us to cast our cares on Him along the way. The Lord expects us to rely on Him for the understanding we need in order to endure any circumstance that we may encounter, for every petition that we have before Him, and as we wait for Him to manifest Himself however, whenever, and wherever He sees fit to do so.

> *Trust in the Lord with all thine heart; and lean not unto thine own understanding. In all thy ways acknowledge him, and he shall direct thy paths.*
>
> PROVERBS 3:5–6

There is one exception to a Christian's level of faith and its correlation to his or her relationship with the Savior: the instantaneous mountain-moving faith of a new Christian. When a sinner is newly saved—becoming a born again Believer—that transformation takes place through faith and confession. One begins to experience what can best be described as a radical sort of faith. The reason for the enormity of the faith level—in what we call baby Christians—is the recollection of where they came from and what it took to get them to the point of salvation. You see, there is only one person who knows exactly how difficult it was to get the Gospel through to you: that one person is you. So faith kicks in as you think, "If God could save me, God can save anybody or God can do anything." For me, even though I abhorred the heartbreaks and many disappointments that I suffered at the hands of others, the struggles as a single mother trying to do it all on my own, and the financial difficulties that I faced on a daily basis, none of that caused me to hate sin enough to let it all go and serve a God who had already invited me to:

> *Cast... [my] care[s] upon him; for he careth for [me].*
>
> 1 PETER 5:7

I thoroughly enjoyed setting and living by my own standards, regardless of how low they were. There is a level of comfort in playing the game called "It's My Life" which is governed by your own rules. When things do not work out as planned, you have the autonomy to change the rules as you go along proclaiming, "Hey, It's

My Life, and I will live it how I want to!" Hence, when you have made yourself your own god, no one can top that but the Master Himself. Consequently, the Bible declares that there is:

> *One Lord, one faith, one baptism. One God and Father of all, who is above all, and through all, and in you all.*
>
> EPHESIANS 4:5–6

When God got that message through to me, and I surrendered my life fully to Him, I was dispatched on a mission for souls to be saved. A level of faith rose up in me that caused me to believe that God could and would save everyone in my path, beginning with my husband. How quickly I had forgotten that it did not happen overnight for me, and I hurriedly discovered that it was not going happen overnight for him either. Rather, I would have to learn how to wait and believe the Word of God that He would save my entire household.

My Initial Wait

My initial encounter with the Lord took place long before I met the angels (Anjie and Martha) that I referred to in chapter one. It was my parents that planted the seed when I was just a little girl being dragged off to Sunday school and witnessing the ruckus in our living room that they referred to as prayer meetings and Bible studies. As I got older (in my teen years), I lost interest in what my parents were trying to instill in me. However, there was a part of me that wanted salvation, just not at that time. When I left home, entering the military, the Lord deliberately put me around those who would be responsible for watering the seed that was already planted inside of me. God used one person in particular: a dear Sister-in-Christ named Tammie. This Tammie was so on fire for God that she went door to door on the military base evangelizing, telling all who she came in contact with about the goodness of Jesus Christ and what He had to offer sinners like myself (at the time). I was so open and receptive that I would let her into my home every time she came by. I never turned her away or pretended as though I was not at home as some did in our neighborhood. I can remember Tammie—patiently and tirelessly—trying to convince me that then was the appointed time for me to take that step into the arms of Jesus. She was ever so serene and tolerant with me as I crossed my legs and spoke to her so matter-of-factly, giving responses like, "I'll get saved one day, but it won't be today." She would just smile, peacefully exit my home, and assure me that she would continue praying for me. Because of where I am in God today, I know that she never defaulted on that promise, providing just enough water to cause that seed to not only survive but to sprout as well. So when I met Anjie, the God that she professed and that is so evident in her life rose up and is responsible for the increase (my acceptance of the Lord into my heart).

[One] planted, [another] watered; but God gave the increase.

1 CORINTHIANS 3:6

Salvation was not an immediate choice for Keith once I accepted Christ into my life. Though he respected my decision, he was not willing to conform to this new lifestyle that I endeavored to pursue. As a matter of fact, this was my first grand experience with waiting on God to answer a major prayer request: to save my husband and deliver him from drugs. I did not realize how agonizing the wait would be. Nor did I realize that He was prepping me for the greater "season of waiting" that was before me. I had no idea what trusting God was really all about. I was now His child, and just like any other spoiled brat, I wanted Him to dry my tears, wrap me in His arms, and give me what I wanted right away. As I mentioned earlier, I thought "If He could save me," this is a piece of cake. To my dismay, it was not as easy as I thought it would be. In fact, at the time I did not expect much to change with Keith, only with myself since I was the one who had made a new commitment. Being caught up in my excitement about God, I neglected to grasp the concept of how real the devil is and how angry he was with me for kicking him to the curb. Therefore, I was blind-sided when he began to attack me through Keith. Once Satan realized that I had slipped through his clutches, he was not about to just usher Keith into the Kingdom of God as well. Satan went full force after his life and his soul.

And the Lord said...behold, Satan hath desired to have you, that he may sift you as wheat. But I have prayed for thee, that thy faith fail not...

LUKE 22:31–32A

Keith's drug addiction progressed, and I was helpless in the situation since I was still away at school. Some months before, he had checked himself into the hospital as an attempt to get help, but he did not follow through with the plan that was presented to him. Even though we were being scrutinized by child protective services for allegations of child neglect while I was in Korea, Keith still could not keep it together. My emotions tempted me to capitalize what he was doing and react to it, but in my heart I knew it was not a matter of whether he cared for his family but rather a matter of control. He had none. Sin had now taken over his life completely, and Satan knew just what bait to offer him: drugs, drugs, and more drugs. He later told me that while he was running the streets and getting high, he was once held up at gun- and knife-point with the very possibility of losing his life. Satan wanted to kill him before God could save him. Also, during the same timeframe he had blown approximately $2,500 of income tax money—which was all we had for our relocation from Georgia to Washington State—in one week on drugs. That alone could be considered an overdose and was enough to take him out for sure. But God!

But God!

Just as I was preparing to graduate from school in Virginia, the battle got quite a bit more intense at the home front. Keith was responsible for cleaning our government quarters in preparation for our move. However, I could not reach him at home, and he would not return any of my calls when I left messages and paged him. This avoidance continued for a space of three consecutive days. Though I was worried about him, I think my anger superseded my concern for his well-being at the time. It was not too long before I shifted my fury from Keith and directed it toward the devil. Righteous indignation arose in me, and I declared war on Satan.

> *And from the days of John the Baptist until now the kingdom of heaven suffereth violence, and the violent take it by force.*
>
> MATTHEW 11:12

Prayer was really new to me, and I had no idea what the term intercession meant. However, a passion rose up in me for my cause: to snatch my husband out of the hands of the enemy. I reached a point of desperation, and I was willing to do whatever I had to do to get what I wanted. I found a place in the barracks (military living quarters) where I could be alone to pray, as I was too embarrassed to even tell my roommate about my situation. As I recall, my prayer was not a very long prayer (maybe about five minutes or so); it is hard to pray much longer than that when you really do not even know how to pray. The only words that I remember verbatim from that prayer are, "God, wherever he is right now, You deal with him and make him call me"! When I got up off of my knees and returned to my room, I did not feel in any way different. Nonetheless, the phone rang within 5 minutes of that prayer, and it was Keith's voice that I heard on the other end. God had heard and answered my prayer, and so expeditiously I might add.

In my distress I called upon the Lord, and cried unto my God: he heard my voice out of his temple, and my cry came before him, even into his ears.

PSALM 18:6

After I got past the shock of God answering my prayer so quickly, I told Keith that I wanted to call him from another phone, as I wanted to speak with him in private. I began to question him about his whereabouts and his actions, and he confessed everything to me without my having to pry for answers. All of a sudden, I grew less concerned with where he was and what he was doing and why he was treating me this way. My heart began to hurt for him, as I felt like he was in a tailspin and did not know how to get out. I began to speak with a level authority that was unfamiliar to me as we discussed his situation—his drug addiction. He could sense that I was not prepared to tolerate it any longer. I told him that I had allowed him to drag that baggage along from state to state and from city to city, but I refused to take it with me to my next duty station. He began to cry and plea with me, asking me not to leave him. I assured him that it was not my intent to leave him. I only wanted him to understand that I had made up my mind about the direction my life was headed. He began to tell me that he wanted to go in the direction that I was going. It was then that I told him, "I am walking with Jesus, and I am not going to stop." He broke down and told me that he was ready to walk with Him too. Keith allowed me to lead him in the sinner's prayer right there over the phone. He was in a phone booth in Georgia, and I was at a pay phone in Virginia. The Omni-present God was there with us both in our respective places. As a result of this experience, Keith likened himself to Superman having gone through a metamorphosis. He went into that phone booth a sinner, and he came out a saint. Glory to the Most High God!

What's the Hold Up With My Stuff?

What you have read are testimonies of what God was faithful to do as a result of the fervent prayers of committed, faith-filled Christians—one was saved for a few years (Tammie), and the other was saved less than two months (myself). This is evidence that God honors every sincere prayer from willing hearts.

> *Then Peter opened his mouth, and said, Of a truth I perceive that* ***God is no respecter of persons:*** *But in every nation he that feareth him, and* ***worketh righteousness****, is accepted with him.*
>
> ACTS 10:34

As children of God, we all have boundless blessings made available to us that are there for the taking. Although these are testimonies about salvation—which is the greatest gift anyone could ever receive—the blessings of the Lord are immeasurable and comes in all forms, shapes, and sizes. God has so much in store for us. Nevertheless, we have to position ourselves to receive the divine promises of God. In order to experience the wonders of God, we have to constantly reevaluate ourselves and where we are in our walk with Him, ensuring that we are in right standing with our Heavenly Father. As a Christian, you should always be aware of the status of your relationship with the Lord, knowing the state of your foundation. Thus, I will conclude this chapter by sharing with you what I believe to be three positions we may find ourselves in that can hinder us from receiving the promises of God. Accordingly, to come out of the holding pattern that you may be in right now might require you to take action—as Tammie and I did—which would cause a divine shift that could potentially put an end to your waiting for what you need or desire from the Lord.

Position #1—You Have Arrived: The holier than thou attitude. Your words are those of self-glorification. You are boastful about your prayer life, how often you fast, and how high you perceive yourself to be in God. You are constantly reminding others of how spiritual you are. You are so into you that you forgot the fact that God commanded you to serve others rather than be self-serving. While you were headed for your destination, you forgot to help someone along the way. As God blessed you, you neglected the charge to be a blessing to someone else. You were so fixated on your destination that you ignored those who were struggling rather than pick them up and take them with you. God would say to you, "If you have arrived, and you are all that, then what do you need from Me?" You have already received your reward—self-exaltation.

For I say, through the grace given unto me, to every man that is among you, not to think of himself more highly than he ought to think;

but to think soberly, according as God has dealt to every man a measure of faith.

ROMANS 12:3

When people puff themselves up, God is reluctant to pour out His blessings upon them for one simple reason: He cannot trust them. God's blessings are accompanied by His glory, and if He cannot trust to bless you, then He is certain that you will mishandle His glory. God is not willing to share His glory with anyone. Now, if the Holy Spirit is tugging at your heart as you read this, apparently this is an area of your life that needs to be yielded to Him. God is a just and forgiving God. It may be tempting to try to brush this off as though it is not for you, thinking of all those whom you feel should be reading this book right now. I would say to you that God is not subjecting you to this revelation for anyone else but you. Thus, I challenge you to take a moment right now to search your heart, allowing God to bring you to a place of repentance for your actions and your thoughts, and permit the ever so gentle Father to cleanse you of your sins. Then he can release you from your holding pattern simultaneously, rendering you qualified to receive everything that He has just for you.

Position #2—Temporarily Off Track: You are in a backslidden state. You were once on fire for God, going along just fine, doing all the right things, and you somehow got distracted. Perhaps it was by the very thing God wants to use to bless you (your marriage, your children, your job, your ministry). It could have been any number of things that caused you to take your focus off of God. The only thing you are certain of is that you found yourself spending more time doing everything but seeking the face of God as you once did. Things have gotten so bad that you are no longer praying or reading your Bible, and your life of fasting is nonexistent. You felt yourself totally slipping away from God, but you could not pick yourself up and get back on track. For some, you may have even found yourself reverting back to your sinful ways. To you I would say, "Good news, help is here for you." The Word of the Lord to you this day is:

> *Turn, O backsliding children, saith the Lord; for I am married unto you: and I will take you one of a city, and two of a family, and I will bring you to Zion: And I will give you pastors according to mine heart, which shall feed you with knowledge and understanding.*
>
> JEREMIAH 3:14–15

You do not have to remain in the rut that you are in. God has prepared a way of escape for you, and it will lead you right back into His loving arms. This is your opportunity to step back onto the pathway to your destiny. Once you are on the right track again, you will be ready to receive all that has been held up and in waiting for you. Once you have returned to your rightful place, ready to live according to the plan God has for your life, it is then that His manifold blessings will overtake you.

> *For the Lord God is a sun and shield: the Lord will give grace and glory: no good thing will he withhold from them that walk uprightly.*
>
> PSALM 84:11

Position #3—Stuck In Curiosity: You have heard about Jesus and all of the benefits of serving Him, but you are just not sure that you are ready to take that step. I assure you that you are more ready than you will ever be. Now I will not promise you that you will not experience any heartaches or pain; but I can, however, assure you that they will never supersede the rewards that you will receive for serving the one true and living God. Regardless of what you endure from this day forth, He will constantly give you peace and remind you that:

> *...all things work together for good to them that love God, to them who are the called according to his purpose.*
>
> ROMANS 8:28

Surely you have been dissatisfied and seeking some way to find fulfillment. You have been looking for all the wrong things in all the wrong places. That which you thought you needed is minute in comparison to Almighty God. He wants to do so much more for you than you can do for yourself. What you have been searching and waiting for has arrived. The Savior not only wants to give you new hope and a new perspective, He wants to give you a new life.

> *Therefore if any man be in Christ, he is a new creature: old things are passed away; behold, all things are become new.*
>
> 2 CORINTHIANS 5:17

When you take this step, what you will experience will certainly top a new house, a new car, a new outfit, or whatever you have been reaching after. My point is: your discontented state is connected with what you have been waiting for. However, what you think you want (or thought that you wanted) is quite different than what you need. Material things bring comfort for a season, but you are in need of a Savior for a lifetime. The awesome thing is that your wait to receive Him can be over instantaneously. The Savior is readily available to you right now. If you are so inclined to put an end to your search right now and a halt to your wait, then re–read the two verses of Scripture (John 3:16 and Romans 10:9) at the beginning of this chapter and read the following prayer with sincerity of heart:

Lord Jesus,

I am a sinner in need of a Savior. I come to You now, asking You to wash me and cleanse me of all my sins. This day I am confessing with my mouth and believing in my heart that You gave your life for me on the cross. It is my belief that you suffered and died on the cross, Father God raised You from the grave, and You are yet still alive. This day, I accept you into my life and into my heart as my Lord and Savior. In Jesus' Name, Amen.

If you have prayed this prayer of salvation, I say to you my Brother, I say to you my Sister, "Welcome to the family. Welcome home Dear One." All of heaven is rejoicing over your soul being saved.

I say unto you, that likewise joy shall be in heaven over one sinner that repenteth, more than over ninety and nine just persons, which need no repentance... Likewise, I say unto you, there is joy in the presence of the angels of God over one sinner that repenteth.

LUKE 15:7

Your next crucial move is to find you a Bible-based church that believes in the same Jesus that you just accepted into your heart. It is imperative for you to find a church home where the Spirit of the Lord is present and the fellowship is sweet. Your wait is finally over; you have received the most important promise—salvation. This one step is just the beginning of you receiving all of the great things God has for you. Enjoy your new life of fulfillment.

Regardless of what position you found yourself in as you read, make the decision to reposition yourself right now as according to the will of God for your life. After you do so, you may sit back and watch the blessings of the Lord begin to pour out and overtake you. You will also have a front row seat to watch the promises of God concerning your destiny be fulfilled right before your eyes. Moreover, you will find that God will freehandedly release those things that you are in waiting for with great anticipation. Reposition yourself now so as to guarantee that you have a sure foundation in your relationship with our Heavenly Father, and expect Him to move for you in ways that only He can!

Chapter 3

Communication Deficiencies

And when he putteth forth his own sheep, he goeth before them, and the sheep follow him: for they know his voice. And a stranger will they not follow, but will flee from him: for they know not the voice of strangers....My sheep hear my voice, and I know them, and they follow me. And I give unto them eternal life; and they shall never perish, neither shall any man pluck them out of my hand. My father, which gave them me, is greater than all; and no man is able to pluck them out of my Father's hand. I and my Father are one.

John 10:4-5; 27-30

Open communication is the key element in every healthy and thriving relationship, whether natural or spiritual in nature. Open communication creates an atmosphere that allows discussion and dialogue; an atmosphere where all parties are given the opportunity to overtly share what is on their hearts, which envelops their deepest and truest thoughts, ideas, opinions, secrets, etc.; an atmosphere that provides assurance, confidentiality, and safety; an atmosphere of harmony, oneness, and unity. As we endeavor to wait before the Lord for His perfect will to be made manifest in our lives, this is the ambiance that He wants us to enjoy—an environment in which we can not only enjoy the comfort of unity that His presence brings, but also one in which we can enjoy one another's presence as well. Open communication, in short, provides an atmosphere in which we can not only sing praises to the Most High God, but as we do so, we can celebrate one another as well as we, together, wait in expectancy and hope in His divine presence.

> *Behold, how good and how pleasant it is for brethren to dwell together in unity!*
>
> PSALM 133:1

Moreover, when open communication is taking place, an atmosphere is created in which all parties get to know one another intimately—becoming keenly familiar with one another's mannerisms, preferences, strengths and weaknesses, and even one another's voice. Given this information, one can evaluate the state of each of his or her relationships of which we are involved in many as fleshly beings. How well are you communicating with your mate? How is your communication with your parents? How about with your children? How about with your siblings? How are you communicating with your pastor (spiritual leader)? Having asked the preceding questions which are all valid and equally important, there is one other that I will pose, which is the most important question of all: How well are you communicating with God, the Father? How you are able to answer this latter question will prove to be a reflection of how you will be able to answer all of the others.

Consequently, how well you communicate with your Heavenly Father is the determinant of the level of intimacy that you will experience in your relationship with Him which literally sets the stage for every other relationship that you have or ever will be involved in. This point regarding relationships is important to note. Reason being is that more often than not, you will find that your seasons of waiting before the Lord will involve those whom you are in some form of relationship with, be it negative or positive. Thus, it is imperative that you are able to openly and effectively communicate with everyone that the Lord allows you to cross paths with, friend or foe. Hence, you must be able to recognize the voice of the Lord in any given direction, instruction, or situation that He places before you.

Furthermore, to ensure that all of the relationships you are involved in are strong and vibrant—even more importantly, God-centered—you must do what it takes to ensure that there are no communication deficiencies in your relationship with Jesus. When you commune with Him daily, as you should, you ought to always ensure that one person is not dominating the conversation every time. If you lead the conversation, be sure to give Him the opportunity to speak back and minister to you and vice versa, if He leads be sure to respond—expediently, obediently, and willingly—to what He is saying to you. In this way, as God gets to know you, you will get to know Him as well and not have to wonder when you hear His still, small voice: Lord, is that really you?

> *And he said, Go forth, and stand upon the mount before the Lord. And, behold, the Lord passed by, and a great strong wind rent the mountains, and brake in pieces the rocks before the Lord; but the Lord was not in the wind: and after the wind an earthquake; but the Lord was not in the earthquake: And after the earthquake a fire; but the Lord was not in the fire: and after the fire a* **still small voice.**
>
> 1 KING 19:11–12

You must not have any preconceived ideas about how the Lord will come or how the Lord will speak, but rather you must be on alert for however He decides to present Himself to you. Yes, indeed He is a great big God, but we all know that often "great things come in small packages." Thus, when He speaks you should be able to differentiate what you are hearing Him say from that which you are hearing from the enemy as he, too, will speak to you in his attempts to override the voice of God. He will do so in order to cause you to stumble or move out of the will of God. Knowing the Good Shepherd's voice without a shadow of a doubt will keep you from making many wrong, hasty decisions; it will keep you from moving outside of the will and the divine timing of God regarding all that concerns you. Knowing His voice will allow you to receive clear instructions for all things that concern you and yours. Knowing His voice will give you that blessed assurance that He is ever–present with you as you are holding on for your long awaited breakthrough. However, you should know that God is not going to force feed you His will. He is a gentle God. He gently knocks on the door to your heart, and He speaks, offering His guidance and fellowship, leaving it laid out before you for the taking.

> *Behold, I stand at the door [as any gentleman should], and knock: if any man hear my voice, and open the door, I will come in to him, and will sup with him, and he with me.*
>
> REVELATION 3:20

Thus, you have to be able to recognize His voice, and be willing to respond to His divine instructions, even if it comes in the form of a single word, such as WAIT! For many, that little four letter word "wait" is like a cuss word, as we live in a "right now" world. However, we have to remember that though we live in this world, as Saints of the Most High God, we are not of the world (See John 17:16). Therefore, our standards/requirements as set by the Master Himself are often different, difficult, and unpopular; however, they are necessary in order to obtain His manifold blessings. Accordingly, should you choose to hearken unto His voice and heed to all that He speaks to you, you will find that the rewards that are certain to follow will be well worth your response to Him. Further, you will find that He will honor His Word, which promises that:

If ye be willing and obedient, ye shall eat the good of the land.

ISAIAH 1:19

[If you would]...seek...first the kingdom of God, and his righteousness [what He requires of you]...all...things shall be added unto you.

MATTHEW 6:33

When there are communication deficiencies in any relationship—especially one's relationship with God—one is certain to miss out on the fulfillment that could be realized in the relationship otherwise. If you engage in effective, efficient, and meaningful communication with Almighty God, you will begin to realize a level contentment and gratification as you have never known it before as you wait on Him, allowing Him to perfect those things which He has in store and is preparing to release into your hands. My challenge to you this day is to re-evaluate the state of your communication and relationship with Him. Do you have any communication deficiencies? Could these deficiencies be barriers between you and what God has for you? Be honest with yourself and with Him about where you really are in your relationship with Him, and endeavor to get to that place He is calling you to. Consider where you may be among the following three types of communication deficiencies. Nevertheless, do not stop at the evaluation process. Rather, set in your heart that you will allow Almighty God to help you overcome whatever communication deficiency you may have, and help you begin to walk in the freshness and freedom of open communication with the Him as He has ordained it to be so.

Communication Deficiency #1—No Communication at All: God is saying to you, "Could you speak up, please. I cannot hear you. In order for me to hear you, you have to say something." The one experiencing this form of deficiency is the one who is not in communication and relationship with the Father at all, lacking a consistent prayer life. You may talk to God sometimes on the go, but you never set aside uninterrupted time to spend with Him. You just sporadically throw out a few words at Him here and there when you need to or when you need something from Him in an instant. It is you whom God is calling to a deeper, more intimate relationship with Him. It is you whom God is wooing to spend time with Him that you may get to know Him better. The very thing that you are waiting for from God is the bait that He is dangling before you saying, "Here it is, here I am; Come and get it, come and get more of Me!"

> *Delight thyself also in the Lord; and he shall give thee the desires of thine heart.*
>
> Psalm 37:4

Not speaking at all is probably just as destructive to a relationship as outright arguing. If no one is speaking, the hidden issues are not exposed, and thus is buried and never dealt with or resolved. It is those issues that you feel you cannot possibly share with anyone at all that God is welcoming you to bring to Him without fear, guilt, or shame. It is when you learn how to lay them at His feet that He will teach you how to articulate them to others in your life, enabling them to understand you and to better respond to all that concerns you.

I'll Speak to Him When He Speaks to Me

Not speaking was the root of the primary dysfunction that Keith and I experienced in our marriage from the onset next to not having Christ in our lives. Because we did not have a relationship with Jesus, it was inevitable that we would have much trouble communicating with one another, especially since neither one of us developed good communication skills in our youth. All we knew when we met each other was that we liked each other a lot, and then we loved each other a lot, and it just seemed like the next step should be marriage. Though we were married in a church by a pastor, we entered our union blindly without any type of premarital counseling (forewarning). Hey! We had figured life and marriage out all on our own. We had determined that we were going to be together forever, and that settled it! That is all good, as that is the glue that caused and yet causes us to hold on to our marriage—in turbulent times—determining not let go. However, it unfortunately does not guarantee joy, peace, and happiness along the way. Thus, many days we were each silently miserable; and neither one of us knew how to break the ice, speak up, and bring to the table those issues that we were in bondage to. We thought that to disagree about anything meant we did not have a good marriage. News Flash: The fact that we did not talk about anything meant that our marriage was in big trouble anyway! We learned this tough lesson through many heartaches and pain, of which most were probably avoidable.

I remember days that Keith said things that hurt my feelings unintentionally or days when he was more quiet than usual, probably just wanting some alone time after a hard day or evening at work. Rather than share my heart with him (when the time was appropriate), with the one who promised to love and to cherish me, I bottled everything all up for safekeeping. Ultimately, I was saying in uncertain words through my actions, "I'll speak to him when he speaks to me!" I would never throw it up in his face verbally, but my actions, demeanor, and my standoffish responses toward him would tell the story all too well. Those things that I never shared with him would turn into insecurities that made me feel like I was not worthy to be talked to, touched, or held. Those things I kept to myself eventually caused me to retreat into my own world, posting abstract signs that declared, "Do Not Disturb!"

Even after we were saved, we did not automatically learn the art of communication. As a matter of fact, after ten years of marriage and all the woes that we have experienced along the way, I confess that we still have a lot to learn. After having endured the devastating blow of a physical and emotional separation, I can admit that had we talked it through (all of it, every single thing), our lives and our marriage would probably have traveled a very different path than it did. Nevertheless, "To God be the glory!" He is using our communication deficiency to educate the Body of Christ for the up-building of His Kingdom. For, as it is in the natural realm, so it is in the spiritual realm.

Try to liken the way I held things from Keith to the way you hold things from God, your Heavenly Father. That is exactly what is happening when you neglect to make time to commune with Him. For each day that passes by and you do not get into His presence, you find that you begin to feel yourself retreating farther and farther away from Him. When you have been away from your prayer closet (place) for a really long time, you begin to feel inadequate and unworthy like maybe God does not even want to hear from you. You know in your heart of hearts that He does, but it is hard not knowing exactly what to say. Well, let me help you by challenging you to get into a quiet place and simply start by saying, "Father, I'm back!" And here is a little something to encourage you. He never left your secret place, you did. He has been waiting there on you all along. Remember He promised:

> *I will never leave thee, nor forsake thee.*
>
> HEBREWS 13:5B

The awesome thing about God is, when you open up and begin to speak to Him, he does not hold a grudge or ignore you. He immediately begins to speak back, ministering to the core of your very soul. He begins to pour out of His goodness into all those barren places in your life. So, I admonish you right now wherever you are to push this manuscript aside, lift your hands to Him as an act of surrender and shout "Daddy, I'm back!" I am certain that He will assure you in His own words, "I'm here. I've been right here all along, waiting just for you!" That is the kind of God we serve, a God of tender mercy and loving kindness.

Communication Deficiency #2—One-sided Communication: God is saying to you, "Can I get a word in? Could you be quiet and listen sometimes? Hey! Don't go. I haven't had My say yet!" Those who are experiencing this form of communication deficiency are likely those who have a set time limit for talking to God. Your prayer time is merely part of a to-do checklist (e.g., wake up [√]; pray 15 minutes [√]; read one Scripture [√]; "Well, I've done my reasonable service for today."). You are so secure in your method and sure that you have satisfied all that is required of you, and thus feel like you deserve to go through each day without difficulty. Sure, you talk to God, but you have not yet discovered that He wants an opportunity to talk back to you. You have not yet learned—or have simply neglected—to wait in His presence long enough to give Him the go ahead to speak a fresh, rhema Word into your spirit. As a result, you have been relying on your own abilities and strength to make it from day to day, many times finding yourself unexplainably discouraged and down trodden, wondering why you always feel so alone when there are people all around. You know that God is near, but you cannot distinguish His voice from all the noise and distractions all around you. The reason you are experiencing this confusion and discontentment is because you have not taken the time to graduate from just talking to Him to diligently seeking His face so that you may get to know Him, to know His voice in your quiet time. You should know that you have been given an appointment, a mandate to:

> *Seek the LORD and his strength, [to] seek his face continually.*
>
> 1 CHRONICLES 16:11

Further, there is a benefit to conscientiously seeking His face giving Him free course to respond to you as only He, the Gentle One can. It takes faith to stay before God with expectancy to hear His voice, to believe that it is not a waste of your time. When you wait in the presence of God, you are saying, "I trust that you are going to meet me here. I believe that you will make it worth my time." When you stay before Him with that confidence and faith–filled expectancy, God swells with eagerness to bless you.

> *But without faith it is impossible to please him: for he that cometh to God must believe that he is, and that he is a rewarder of them that diligently seek him.*
>
> HEBREWS 11:6

Be encouraged in knowing that you are getting there, to your rightful place of fellowship and intimacy with Him. You are already talking to Him which is the first step. Now are you willing to take the next step which is making the time to wait in His presence so that

He can talk to you that you may come to really know Him? Should you do so, you will find that an opening will be created for Him to pour into you His Words of affirmation and approval, His directions and instructions, His power and strength. You will discover a fulfillment in your life and walk with Jesus that you have never known before. I give my personal guarantee that you will not be disappointed, as you will come to feel the fullness of joy in His presence (See Psalm 16:11). Moreover, you will find that you can tap into your direct line of communication with Him regarding all those things that He has and is doing just for you. Dare to spend just a little more time with Him, getting to know of His goodness, His love, and His mercy. I promise you will discover a longing for more just as King David did who says:

> *O taste and see that the LORD is good: blessed is the man that trusteth in him.*
>
> PSALM 34:8

Communication Deficiency #3—Disgruntled Communication (Arguing Your Case with God): God is saying to you, "Don't you know that your arms are too short to box with me? And surely you know you could never outrun me. When I speak, I expect you to move in whatever direction I point you—without wondering, without hesitation, without lip service, and without excuses. I haven't changed my mind about what I have called you to do. So, please don't question Me!" Remember, this is He, the One who spoke and an entire universe was formed with you now abiding in it. You may think that you know what is best for you from time to time, but be reminded that you serve the Omniscient, All-knowing God. You have to learn how to give up your right to be right, especially when it comes to Him. Why? Because God always has the last Word and the last laugh.

I am sure He often finds humor in the fact that we sometimes think we know better than Him what is best for us, that we can take care of our situations better and faster than He can, forgetting to allow Him to be the Vindicator that He is very capable of being for us. The one who experiences this form of communication deficiency is one who hears and acknowledges the voice of God for the most part, but tries to reason with God, attempting to convince Him to change His mind about what He has already spoken to you. You tend to look at your circumstances or your current situation and determine that there must be a better time for God to use you, or maybe He should just use someone else for now. After all, going through takes a toll on a person, as it tends to blur or sway one's vision. Furthermore, it seems to clog one's spiritual ears—in a sense—as you sometimes begin to ignore or blot out God's Word, which says:

> *God is not a man, that he should lie; neither the son of man, that he should repent: hath he said, and shall he not do it? or hath he spoken, and shall he not make it good?*
>
> NUMBERS 23:19

The fact that you go through trials and tribulations neither releases you from the calling of God nor affords you the opportunity to take a vacation from it. So, rather than wrestle with God, just yield to Him, acknowledge Him, and hearken unto His voice. In order to hear Him clearly, you must settle yourself down and be at ease in His presence rather than try to figure Him out or a way out of what He whispers into your spirit instructing you on what to do. Determine to totally submit to His will, whatever it may be, as you will come to realize that His plan for your life is perfect and tailor made explicitly for you.

The flip side of this deals with the one who is not trying to persuade God to change His mind but rather trying to rush Him to make it happen. Having heard the call, you want to bypass preparation—which more often than not comes in the form of tests and trials. You are saying, "Come on God, let me go now. Use me now, Lord!" God is saying to you, "Listen, you are not ready yet. You haven't been through anything yet." You, Dear One, should know that going through tests will prepare you for what is ahead in your walk with God. They will ready you for what is ahead of you in the future. So do not try to force God to release you sooner than you are ready to step out. Let Him equip you.

But the God of all grace, who hath called us unto his eternal glory by Christ Jesus, after that ye have suffered a while, make you perfect, stablish, strengthen, settle you.

1 PETER 5:10

Allow Him to fully equip you for what He has destined for you to do. He already knows what you need to take you through the race that He will enter you into.

Getting weary or restless in the wait could cause you to slumber or move ahead of God, which could eventually lead you away from the things of God, causing you to do what is not pleasing to Him only to please the flesh for a moment. It is then that you must be careful to talk to and with Him and not at Him. Do not get caught up in the way that things look or seem from your own perspective. Learn how to see things through the eyes of God by humbling yourself before Him so that He can show you and tell you how to move and when to move, and more importantly what is and is not of Him.

> *While we look not at the things which are seen, but at the things which are not seen: for the things which are seen are temporal; but the things which are not seen are eternal.*
>
> 2 CORINTHIANS 4:18

> *For we walk by faith, not by sight.*
>
> 2 CORINTHIANS 5:7

Oft times it is hard to change old habits and old ways of doing things. However, I challenge those of you who are experiencing this communication deficiency to try a different approach with God, and watch Him prove that He is very capable of being the Head of the Steering Committee for your future, for your life, and for your family

and ministry. Dare to let go and let God this day. Dare to be quiet before Him, allowing Him to speak to you as only He can in a whisper that will, likewise, teach you how to be "swift to hear, slow to speak, and slow to wrath" (See James 1:19), giving you peace in knowing that God has it all in control.

To Know Him

Now if I had to sum up the reasons for anyone having either of these three communication deficiencies all into one compound issue, I would have to say that they each revolve—in some way—around not truly knowing God, not knowing who He really is. With that, I believe I can safely say those who are struggling in their communication with Him are also struggling with whether they, in fact, know this awesome God that they profess to serve. This lack of confidence in your relationship with Him is probably connected to something more than not communing with Him verbally as you should. For many, you have not been diligently tapping into another source of communication that is available to us, His children, which is arguably the best way to get to know Him. Do not forget that you have His Word which is the purest and clearest depiction of who He really is.

> *In the beginning was the Word, and the Word was with God, and the word was God.*
>
> John 1:1

This Scripture lets us know that if we really want to get to know Him, we have to know His Word. Everything we need to know about Him, we can find it in His Word. Everything we need to know about how to live, we can find it in His Word. What He has in store for us, we can discover it in His Word. How he wants to move, we can find the directions in His Word. The way we get to know Him and everything about Him, is by going to His Word.

Thus, we are without excuses. No more can it be said, "He doesn't speak to me. I can't hear Him with all that is going on with and around me." God is speaking to you, and all you have to do is go to His Word in order to find out what He has already been saying to you. As I mentioned earlier, He has not changed His mind or His person.

> *Jesus Christ [is] the same yesterday, and to day, and for ever.*
>
> HEBREWS 13:8

Should you decide to take on the challenge of getting into His Word so that you can get to know Him all the more, you will find that your entire relationship with Him will be totally transformed. You will come to know Him and the power of His resurrection as you could never have imagined otherwise (See Philippians 3:10). You will come to know and hear His voice more clearly as you should. You will come to enjoy the intimacy of knowing all about the One whom you have been calling your Savior all along. When you get to know Him, then you will long to communicate with Him as you should. You will long to meet with Him in a way that you not only talk with Him, but that you may hear Him talk back to you saying words like, "Here my Son. Here my Daughter. Here my Child. Here is what I have had waiting for you all the time."

Part 2

The Heart of the Matter

It is never easy to walk through times of testing even though we know God will work out all things for our good (See Romans 8:28). However, we must come to the realization that trials come to establish us in the Kingdom of God. Though trials come, and come they will, God will uphold us through each and every one. We must go through, but it is always His plan to bring us out with greater fortitude. God is so gracious that, as we go through, He accompanies us. He says that we are to:

> *Fear thou not; for I am with thee: be not dismayed; for I am thy God: I will strengthen thee; yea, I will help thee; yea, I will uphold thee with the right hand of my righteousness.*
>
> ISAIAH 41:10

> *And he said unto me, My grace is sufficient for thee: for my strength is made perfect in weakness. Most gladly therefore will I rather glory in my infirmities, that the power of Christ may rest upon me.*
>
> 2 CORINTHIANS 12:9

Chapters 4–6 discuss much about going through, but will enlighten you on the proper etiquette as you are in the midst of tribulation. These chapters emphasize how necessary it is to be aware of our actions and behaviors while enduring things which God

does not essentially subject us to, but allows us to go through. Paul reminds us that we must:

> *...endure hardness, as a good soldier of Jesus Christ.*
>
> 2 TIMOTHY 2:3

As you read the following three chapters, it is imperative that you do so with an open heart in order for God to get through to you whatever message He needs to. Allow Him to openly reveal to you where you fit into each of these pages. The very areas that God needs to minister to in your life are directly related to the hold up of that which you desire for God to release to you, or better yet what our loving God desires to give to you.

Chapter 4

Love Rations: Rational Love

Thou shalt have no other gods before me...
for I the LORD thy God am a jealous God...
Exodus 20:3, 5

For thou shalt worship no other god: for the LORD,
whose name is Jealous, is a jealous God...
Exodus 34:14

One thing we must be mindful of at all times with God is that there is a place in our hearts that He is unwilling to share with anyone or anything else. We must understand and recognize that there is a position that He considers to be justly, rightfully, and solely His. Just in case anyone reading this has uncertainty about what place God wants to hold in our hearts and our lives, it is first place. Further, He does not take too kindly to anyone who deviates from this order. It is not in His nature to accept leftovers; He wants our best, the first fruits of our lives. Our act of placing Him first is our way of acknowledging that we belong to Him wholly and completely. This act gives God what He rightfully deserves—the discretion to share us however and with whomever He pleases. In the following Scripture, God makes it clear, without question, that He owns us outright.

> *What? know ye not that your body is the temple of the Holy Ghost which is in you, which ye have of God, and ye are not your own? For ye are bought with a price: therefore glorify God in your body, and in your spirit, which are God's.*
>
> 1 CORINTHIANS 6:19–20

It is simple! We belong to God and not ourselves. We are His property, and we do not have the authority to ration out any part of our being however we see fit. It may seem rational to the carnal mind to love your spouse more than life itself or to put your children or parents on pedestals; but there is a danger zone here. We are to love those who are a part of our lives with agape (unconditional) love; however, we must do so through the love of God and not more than we love God Himself. Our love for others should be enhanced by, but not compete with our love for Him.

> *Jesus said unto him, Thou shalt love the Lord thy God with all thy heart, and with all thy soul, and with all thy mind. This is the first and great commandment. And the second is like unto it, Thou shalt love thy neighbour as thyself.*
>
> MATTHEW 22:27–39

This Scripture clearly depicts the expectation that God has for us with regard to our love for Him and others. He comes first. It is through our pure love for Him, as He has mandated and ordained for it to be expressed toward Him, that we acquire the ability to love others as we should (our spouses, our children, our parents, our siblings, our pastors and leaders, our friends, and even strangers, just to name a few). Also, when our love for God is in its proper perspective, it leaves no room for us to set up other idols in our lives such as: that job or promotion that we must have, that position in ministry that we have been waiting on for too long, the business that would cause us to sacrifice everything just to get it off the ground, the husband or wife that we cannot wait another day for God to put in our path, that thing that I have been waiting for God to release for far too long, and the list can go on and on. You know what has the potential to rise up and attempt to take the place of God in your life. Beware, as the Scripture warns us that He will not tolerate anyone who would dare to put any god before Him. Remember when we put God in the forefront, that provokes Him to bless us immeasurably (See Matthew 6:33).

A Rude, Yet Necessary Awakening

Allow me to show you how one can unconsciously create a god and not be aware of being in direct violation of God's warning that He will not allow us to put another god before Him. In my case, unbeknownst to me, I had somehow made Keith my god in that I had

come to love my husband more than I loved God Himself. Oh, what a rude awakening this was for me. During the time of separation from my husband, God personally gave me this revelation (wake-up call) at a time that I least expected to learn such a thing about myself and where things really stood in my relationship with Him. God is quite clever in how he chooses the most inopportune time (for us) but the perfect time for Him to cause us to see ourselves for who we really are at any given moment. In short, He knows exactly how to and when He can get our undivided attention. He recognizes when we are in a state of unconscious toward Him for far too long, and He knows how to shake us and cause us to arise from whatever slumber we find ourselves in at the divinely appointed time.

> *And that, knowing the time, that now it is high time to awake out of sleep: for now is our salvation nearer than when we believed.*
>
> ROMANS 13:11

It was about two or three months into my separation from Keith that grief set in. His actions and his words would often leave me incapacitated for weeks at a time. There were days that I literally felt that I did not have the physical ability to remove myself from my bed. I had resorted to closing the dark curtains in my room which would remain that way for days at a time. I had graduated from community college in June of 2003, and I had transferred to a university to pursue my goal of attaining my bachelor's degree in accounting. So, the depression that I was experiencing at the time was posing a major problem for me. Aside from school, I was the president of the women's ministry at my church, and I was heavily involved in ministry outside of my local church as well. Oh yeah, did I mention that I was solely responsible for caring for our three minor children during this season as well? The weight of it all caused me to back away from all that was ever so important and meaningful in my life.

Though I had not made the declaration, "I Quit!," that is ultimately what I had intuitively done. My heart ached so bad, that I wished I could just stay asleep until God would come, gently nudge me, and say, "Yolanda, it's over, you can get up and move on now." I suppose I was trying to accomplish that every time I pulled the covers over my head. Sadly, I have to report that my agony and misery did not just dissipate as I slept away my days and nights. Now that I think about it, even though I had the dark curtains closed and my covers over my head, I could not sleep very much at all. In that darkness, I had a major battlefield going on in my mind and my spirit as the enemy attempted to extend my season of despair, thus rendering me incapable of doing what God had called me to do—be a mouthpiece for Him.

Do not misunderstand me, as I am not saying that we can or should just shirk grief and keep moving as if nothing is happening at all. We are in the flesh, and our flesh does respond negatively to those traumatic circumstances we encounter. Nonetheless, we must not permit our grief to shift gears into a pity party for an indefinite period of time. That is where I, in due course, found myself. Correction: that is where the Lord found me, got my attention, and made me realize that it was time to move back into the place He had called me to be in—a place of witnessing and worshiping as I was in waiting for Him to move in my situation. When I received the clarion call from the Lord to awake out of my sleep, I learned a very important lesson: that grief is not an excuse to deviate from the plan of God for my life, regardless of how bad it hurts. Even when I am in pain, there are still sinners in need of hearing about a Savior, and I am responsible for telling them about the One who rescued me. God was able to convince me that my willingness to do it His way—witnessing and worshiping—would reap greater rewards than staying in bed. He also assured me that if I were to be obedient to Him, by putting Him first, that He would make it well "*Worth the Wait!*" Guess What? He was true to His promise.

Love Me...Love Me Not

In my case, God came to my rescue by way of a confrontation or provocation so to speak. When God speaks, He has a way of doing so with a sense of purpose in order to challenge or to provoke us in some way. His Word is never idle, but rather it comes on divine assignment to bring us to a point of self-recognition. I am reminded of how Jesus interrogated Simon Peter about whether he loved Him. I can certainly empathize with Simon Peter in that I am very familiar with the Father suggesting that my love for Him was not what I thought it to be. In a moment I will give the accounts of how God confronted me regarding my love for Him, but for now let us look briefly at an encounter that Simon Peter had with the Lord.

> *...Jesus saith to Simon Peter, Simon,...lovest thou me more than these? He saith unto him, Yea, Lord; thou knowest that I love thee. He saith unto him, Feed my lambs. He saith unto him again the second time, Simon,...lovest thou me? He saith unto him, Yea, Lord; thou knowest that I love thee. He saith unto him, Feed my sheep. He saith unto him the third time, Simon,...lovest thou me? Peter was grieved because he said unto him the third time, Lovest thou me? And he said unto him, Lord, thou knowest all things; thou knowest that I love thee. Jesus saith unto him, Feed my sheep.*
>
> JOHN 21:15–17

Would you allow me to tamper with the thought process of Simon during this line of questioning? When Jesus asked whether Simon loved Him the first time, Simon was probably comfortable at this stage of the interrogation. Perhaps he perceived that it was a fair and innocent question, that Jesus just wanted some assurance that his heart was in the right place. Not only did Simon, in all confidence, answer Jesus with assertion that he does love Him, but he implied that Jesus was aware of his love ("thou knowest that I love thee"). Jesus gave Simon a directive to feed His sheep, but He then repeated the same thought-provoking question. At this point, I can imagine that Simon was becoming slightly irritated or unnerved by this time, but without hesitation, he answered the question in the same manner. Uh, oh! Much to Simon's dismay, Jesus was not yet satisfied with the response; He inquired of Simon's love for Him a third and final time.

This time, I am sure Simon was frustrated as he pointed out to Jesus that He is all–knowing, and thus should know that he loves Him. The Scripture also reveals the fact that Jesus asking the same question three times brought Simon grief. Imagine with me the parade of thoughts going on in Simon Peter's mind for a moment: "*Surely, Jesus is not deaf because He is Jehovah Rophe, God who heals. Surely, He did not misunderstand me the first two times, as He is omniscient, God who knows all things. So, if the problem does not lie within Jesus, hmmm, it must lie within me.*" Simon was forced to do some soul searching on the spot which at times can bring about disappointing results when one sees alarming truths about oneself.

As with Simon, our feathers may get a little ruffled from time to time when Father God begins to deal with questionable matters in our lives, causing us to come to a point of self–realization. Often we have to acknowledge some things that we never imagined we would discover about ourselves—such as having idols in our lives that we unconsciously esteem higher than our Heavenly Father. It is not that God wants to tantalize us by showing us our inner shortcomings; He does so to give us the opportunity to deal with them so that we may be able to bring our lives in alignment with His Word. It is then that we can reap the full benefits of serving Him and position ourselves to receive of His goodness—which contains our long–awaited breakthroughs. When we walk according to God's will for us, there is nothing that He will keep back from us, as He longs to bless us (See Psalm 84:11).

Oh No God... I Love You More

Here is my story of how God called me to attention. On my bed of grief, where I had camped out, God began to speak to me. I was in such distress, that I felt like I could not even pray. I guess I was relying on the residue of prayers I had stored up during the times I spent on the mountaintop (when all was well in my life). Sometimes my heart ached so bad, I could not even bring myself to open my mouth and say anything to God. It was not intentional, but I had digressed to the point of not going to my prayer place at all. In a sense, I had moved my altar into my master bedroom. Any conversation I was having with God during that time was happening from my bed. Most often I could only moan in my spirit. Sometimes I just curled up in the fetal position hoping that it would all be over really soon. Other times I cried and wailed and, from time to time I mustered up the words, "Lord, help me!" Today I rejoice as I say, helped me, He did.

In my distress I cried unto the LORD, and he heard me.

PSALM 120:1

God interrupted my pity party by making the following statement: "You love Keith more than you love me!" I was stunned at His accusation, so I responded by requesting Him to repeat what He had said. This time He said, "You love your husband more than you love me!" Of course I denied His claim over and over again as I tried to explain myself and how I was feeling, but all to no avail. In tears, I went back and forth trying to convince God that I love Him more than anything, that I did love Him more than I love my husband. I was devastated, but I eventually accepted the mere fact that I was not winning that tug-o-war with God.

I was so insistent that God had to spell it out to me, and that was more devastating than Him merely bringing to my attention that I was shortchanging Him by putting Keith first. The Lord began to itemize my actions that were indicative of me putting my husband before Him. He began to point out to me the facts of the matter, that if He were first in my life I would not still be wallowing in my bed of misery after several months had passed, but rather be found doing what He had called me to do—minister to His people. To have God wash my face with this chastisement/rebuke seemed unbearable at first. However, while it traumatized me, it transformed me as well enabling me to put things into perspective in the midst of my trial. God loves us enough to mention the hard things that would expose, to us, the truth and the loving-kindness that He feels toward us.

O Lord, correct me, but with judgment; not in thine anger, lest thou bring me to nothing.

JEREMIAH 10:24

For whom the Lord loveth he correcteth; even as a father the son in whom he delighteth.

PROVERBS 3:12

Though God was forceful in making me come to terms with how I was slacking spiritually, He was also gentle and compassionate as He assured me that He still has my situation under control. He only needed me to get past my flesh (feelings) so that I could rise above my state of affairs and eventually get my relationship back on track with Him. What I realized in this instance is that I had become so consumed by what I was hoping and praying for that I had, all along, been neglecting the One who would be responsible for giving me my heart's desire. I had made my desire (the hope of my husband's return home) my god. This was unacceptable in the sight of the Lord whether I could see it or not. As a matter of fact, when I was oblivious to the matter, God stepped in and shined His light on it for me to see. His action motivated me to get up, dust myself off, and get back in the race.

> *Wherefore seeing we also are compassed about with so great a cloud of witnesses, let us lay aside every weight, and the sin which doth so easily beset us, and let us run the race that is set before us, Looking unto Jesus the author and finisher of our faith...*
>
> HEBREWS 12:1–2A

We must come to realize that going through is not ultimately about the situation at hand. God often allows the peculiar things to come before us as a reality check from time to time. It is not all about us. Others are watching us to learn the true character of this Jesus that we profess. God would not permit us to be a stumbling block for others who need to know Him. We are required to stand firm and walk upright before Him, and often times it does require us to look to Him (the Holy One) for the endurance and faith that we need. When He is the center of our focus—when we put Him first—we are able to trust Him with hardly any effort at all.

Right now I would like to challenge you. You, too, should examine yourself just to be sure that you are not consumed by what you want from God, which would mean you are in threat of making your ambition your god. Ask yourself questions such as:

- How much time do I spend thinking about my situation, my trial, my desire?
- Am I consumed by my thoughts of what I want to take place in my life?
- Are my prayers well balanced, or are they saturated with my personal requests?
- When I read my Bible, am I distracted by thoughts about my circumstances?
- Can I go at least 1 hour without thinking about my problem?
- Do I think about my situation more than I think about God?

If you find "you", "your desires", "your thoughts", or "your desired end" to be the focal point of your answers, there is a slight chance that you have God on the back burner in your life. However, you should not let guilt grip you because of your discovery. Praise God that you do not have to live in self-deceit any longer. You should be careful to not allow yourself to enter into self-condemnation either. God is gracious and merciful, and that is not His purpose for revealing to you the true contents of your heart. Remember His Word which says:

> *There is therefore now no condemnation to them which are in Christ Jesus, who walk not after the flesh, but after the Spirit.*
>
> ROMANS 8:1

As with me, God only wants to get you to your proper placement in Him in preparation for the great things that are before you. Your untainted love for Him will guarantee your receipt of what He has for you at the appointed time.

Chapter 5

Back to the Potter's Wheel

And the vessel that he made of clay was marred in the hand of the potter: so he made it again another vessel, as seemed good to the potter to make it. Then the word of the Lord came to me saying, O house of Israel, cannot I do with you as the potter? saith the Lord. Behold, as the clay is in the potter's hand, so are ye in mine hand, O house of Israel.

Jeremiah 18:4–6

A day or so after I was called into ministry to preach the Gospel, I was at a retreat strolling alongside the waters at Pacific Beach, Washington. At the time, I had only been walking with the Lord for a relatively short period of time, as I had received salvation just a little over a year earlier. As I looked out into the deep waters, something was taking place in the depth of my spirit, causing me to make a request in prayer that I had never petitioned

God about before. To be more precise, I had no control over the utterance of words that I spoke to the Lord in that instance. My words to God that day were "Lord, I want you to strip me down and build me back up again." At the time I said it, I did not consider for a moment what that actually meant. To be honest, as a baby Christian I thought it sounded pretty good to me. You know, it sort of had a little ring to it. Oblivious to the true meaning of what I had just asked God to do to me, I was excited about my prayer life going to a new level.

The aforementioned request was made during my personal prayer time; so I did not feel compelled to share that experience with anyone else who was attending the retreat with me. Something amazing happened later on during a group session as we were preparing to get into the Word. While in prayer, getting ready to start our discussion, one of the ladies under the unction of the Holy Spirit started to speak a prophetic word to all of us. Her words were as follow: "God says He is going to strip us down and build us back up again!" She said it with such force and surety. At the time of this experience, I had never really been exposed to prophecy in this way; so this was remarkable to me. I sobbed uncontrollably for quite a while during that setting. I was in awe of the fact that the very same words that I spoke to the Lord could be repeated by someone that I had not shared it with. It was enlightening for me to discover that I was, in fact, hearing the voice of God in prayer. However, at that moment I somehow sensed that learning what this meant would probably bring about some less than pleasurable circumstances as I endeavored to serve the Lord with a pure heart. God was getting ready to begin the purification process in me, to do just what I asked Him to do. Suddenly the word "strip" was being illuminated in the mind of my spirit; but it no longer seemed appealing to say the least. Nevertheless, I came to grips with the fact that I would be willing to undergo whatever necessary spiritual renovations to attain the promises that God has for me. I sure hope that you are willing too.

Under Spiritual Construction

I have come to learn that sanctification is a life long process, and we have to strive for it every single day. The Holy Spirit is so gentle that He does not force change upon us, but rather leaves it up to us to submit to it. From time to time we must take on the spirit of David who recognized his need for change and pleaded with the Lord to make him anew. David's cry to the Lord was:

> *Create in me a clean heart, O God; and renew a right spirit within me.*
>
> PSALM 51:10

I am convinced that our Heavenly Father has a burning desire to do that, just so we can be all He created us to be and have all that He desires to give to us. He says:

A new heart also will I give you, and a new spirit will I put within you: and I will take away the stony heart out of your flesh, and I will give you an heart of flesh.

EZEKIEL 36:26

Those who have already accepted Christ as Lord and Savior can all probably attest to this one thing: even after salvation, one still has behaviors and tendencies that conflict with being a born again Christian. After the excitement and zeal that one receives upon accepting Christ begins to plateau somewhat, old habits sometimes begin to manifest. Now, this troubles the new Believer, and rightly so. It is a natural aspiration to please God that causes such convictions, and this is good. Nonetheless, choosing to serve Christ does secure us a place in heaven, but unfortunately it does not render us perfect. We must still live here on this earth in the flesh until we go on to glory. Moreover, we have to realize that God alone can change or take away those things that are not pleasing to Him, and He will if we ask and allow him to—if we surrender all of it to Him. As with David, He will honor our appeals for Him to:

Purge…[us] with hyssop, and…[we] shall be clean: wash…[us], and…[we] shall be whiter than snow.

PSALM 51:7

Allow David to be an encouraging example that when God has a plan for you, He will do whatever is necessary to get you into shape and mold you into what He wants you to be. The awesome thing about God, the Father is that He does not judge us for who we are and where we currently are in our relationship with Him. He focuses on who He created us to be—the end product (See Jeremiah 1:5a). The Lord Jesus is so compassionate that He graciously and patiently loves us beyond our faults, allowing us to fall over and over again until we reach whatever level He ordains for us to be at in Him. We can find encouragement in the Word which states:

> *For a just man falleth seven times and riseth up again...*
>
> PROVERBS 24:16A

In this very thing, we can be confident that God is for us and not against us. Because of the purpose He has for us, our God of all grace permits us to stumble until we find our balance on the way to what He has prepared for us. He works with us right where we are as we move step by step, toward the high calling in Christ Jesus. And the Everlasting Father takes pleasure in laboring with us until we become the vessels of honor that He made us to be. Behold His promise that:

> *If a man therefore purge himself... he shall be a vessel unto honour, sanctified, and meet for the master's use, and prepared unto every good work.*
>
> 2 TIMOTHY 2:21

I am so grateful, as we all should be, that even whilst under spiritual reconstruction God's mercy is ever so present with us. More often than not, we are harder on ourselves than God would

ever be for things that we do and errors that we make. Because of His goodness and mercy, He deserves our praise.

> *O Give thanks unto the Lord; for he is good: for his mercy endureth for ever.*
>
> PSALM 136:1

> *It is of the Lord's mercies that we are not consumed, because his compassions fail not. They are new every morning: great is [His] faithfulness.*
>
> LAMENTATION 3:22–23

You see, we tend to set higher standards for ourselves than God does, allowing guilt and self–condemnation to grip us when we fail. To fail does not mean that all is lost. Further, we must realize that no one is perfect, and we should not sanction the enemy to discourage us when we miss the mark every now and then. We are human, and the Bible declares that:

> *There hath no temptation taken you but such that is common to man: but God is faithful, who will not suffer you to be tempted above that ye are able; but will with the temptation also make a way to escape, that ye may be able to bear it.*
>
> 1 CORINTHIANS 10:13

God, in His infinite wisdom, will teach us how and enable us to overcome those things we struggle with that are not pleasing to Him. Sure we will err, but He only expects us to repent and learn from

our mistakes, not dwell in or on them. As we endeavor to walk with Him according to His Word, He will in turn honor our efforts to please Him by rewarding us—by releasing His promises to us.

Broken to Be Made Whole

Consider the job of one whose profession is demolition—tearing things down in preparation to rebuild. There are times the entire structure of a building must be destroyed and removed from its site to behold the masterpiece that will be built to replace it. What is wrong with the old building? Could not a few repairs bring it up to par? Maybe a couple of cans of paint, some new carpeting, and window dressings to improve its appearance? Sometimes it takes quite a bit more than just a few improvements in order to realize the true value of a thing. It is not that the old building is completely useless; it just does not complement the vision of the new one. Take notice of the following words Jesus spoke to His disciples:

> *And he spake also a parable unto them; No man putteth a piece of a new garment upon an old; if otherwise, then both the new maketh a rent, and the piece that was taken out of the new agreeth not with the old. And no man putteth new wine into old bottles; else the new wine will burst the bottles, and be spilled, and the bottles shall perish. But new wine must be put into new bottles; and both are preserved.*
>
> LUKE 5:36–38

If you look closely at these verses of Scripture, you will see a correlation to the theory of the purpose for demolition. God

knows that the old things of our past can only serve as hindrances to what He wants to accomplish in our present and future. That is why we must:

> *...put off the old man with his deeds; And...put on the new man, which is renewed in knowledge after the image of him that created him...*
>
> COLOSSIANS 3:9B–10

Is it easy to walk in the way of the Lord? No. Not with the temptations that we face every day. Does it feel good going through the process of being shaped and molded, as if in the hands of the potter? Not even a little bit. All the same, God says that we are in His hands as the clay is in the potter's hand. He will not be satisfied with the slightest mar or blemish in our character. Therefore, as His work in progress, He intends to break each of us down and rebuild us until He sees in us what He is looking for—Himself.

> *So God created man in his own image, in the image of God created he him; male and female created he them.*
>
> GENESIS 1:27

From this we learn that God can create a masterpiece out of our brokenness if we allow Him. In essence, true surrender to God occurs when we are broken down to our lowest state. God also considers it to be a sacrifice, which pales in comparison to the great sacrifice that Jesus made on Calvary. He beckons us in this manner:

I beseech thee therefore, brethren, by the mercies of God, that ye present your bodies a living sacrifice, holy, acceptable unto God, which is your reasonable service. And be not conformed to this world: but be ye transformed by the renewing of your mind, that ye may prove what is that good, and acceptable, and perfect, will of God.

ROMANS 12:1–2

The sacrifices of God are a broken spirit: a broken and a contrite heart, O God, thou wilt not despise.

PSALM 51:17

Even though this tends to leave us vulnerable, we must remember that God will handle us with the ultimate care as He strategically reviews His blueprints for our lives. His aim is to reshape us into someone whom we never thought we could be. As with the potter, God is after perfection, and He does not have a "that will do" attitude when it comes to us, His children. We ought to be the same way, dissatisfied with anything less than the perfect will of God for our lives. Thus, we should look beyond what it means to be broken in the hands of God and trust Him to dazzle us with His finished product.

Let us envision a potter who has spent all day long working on a piece of art, and he or she gets to the end of the day only to find that his or her favorite piece of art has a slight, hairline crack in it. I am sure that you can imagine the disgust or disappointment that the potter will feel after taking so much care to ensure perfection, to find that his or her prized possession is marred. Now the potter has a couple of options:

> **Option #1:** To accept his outcome of the piece as is; turn the piece around on the shelf so that it cannot be seen by the public eye. After all, it is just a slight flaw that is hardly visible to the naked eye at all.
>
> **Option #2:** Consider what he sees, recognize it for what it really is (not the desired end that he or she had hoped for), cut his or her losses, crumble it up, and start all over again until he or she gets the desired outcome.

Now a professional potter, who is not doing it just as a hobby will choose option number two. He, like our Heavenly Father, will not settle for second best. Now I suggested that the potter would react this way toward a favored piece of art. So, too, will the Master toward us.

Each of us in our own right is God's favorite child. He has more than enough favor to go around. So, as the Scripture suggests in the heading of this chapter, we are as the clay is in the Potter's hand. Therefore, he will continue to work on us and with us until He can finally see the "you and me" that He always knew that we could be. God will never just accept us as is. It does not matter how much time He has already invested into us; he will break us down, starting over again and again. He alone knows His plan for us, and He will endure with us until He realizes it.

For we are his workmanship, created in Christ Jesus unto good works, which God hath before ordained that we should walk in them.

EPHESIANS 2:10

Just Embrace the Process

Understand that it is a given that brokenness often brings about pain and can prove to be distressful at times; but it is the outcome that we must focus on, not the process. The mere fact that God is willing to endure with us should be convincing enough for us to submit to the process regardless of the discomfort we may experience. Our God expects us to embrace the process regardless of its intensity, and continue on through it. His command:

Thou therefore endure hardness, as a good soldier of Jesus Christ.

2 TIMOTHY 2:3

To avoid brokenness is almost as if we are placing ourselves above Jesus who experienced it in its supreme form—death by crucifixion. And even if that example is too extreme to grasp, consider what God allowed Job to endure. Though He had no idea why God would suffer him to undergo such heartache and turmoil in his life, he submitted to it nonetheless. Walk with me through a bit of Job's experience with brokenness.

And the Lord said unto Satan, Hast thou not considered my servant Job, that there is none like him in the earth, a perfect and an upright man, one that feareth God, and escheweth evil? And Satan answered and said,

Doth Job fear God for nought?...put forth thine hand now, and touch all that he hath, and he will curse thee to thy face...And the Lord said unto Satan, Behold, all that he hath is in thy power; only upon himself put not forth thy hand...And there came a messenger unto Job, and said, The oxen were plowing, and the asses were feeding: And the [enemy] fell upon them, and took them away...slain their servants...burned up the sheep...fell upon the camels...Thy sons and thy daughters were eating and drinking in their eldest brother's house: And there came a great wind...and smote the four corners of the house, and it fell upon the young men, and they are all dead...Then Job arose, and rent his mantle, and shaved his head, and fell down upon the ground, and worshipped. And said, Naked came I out of my mother's womb, and naked shall I return thither: the Lord gave, and the Lord hath taken away; blessed be the name of the Lord. In all this Job sinned not, nor charged God foolishly.

JOB 1:8–22

In short, Job embraced the process without any understanding of why he had to go through it or any foresight as to how he would come out of it. There is so much we can learn from the character of Job when we are subjected to those things which we consider to be unbearable in our lives. Surely the accounts of Job's trials can encourage us that it is not about us, but rather the One who created us. We must worship Him in the midst of our storms as Job did with certainty that it will be worth it in the end.

Behold, we count them happy which endure. Ye have heard of the patience of Job, and have seen the end of the Lord: that the Lord is very pitiful, and of tender mercy.

JAMES 5:11

And the Lord turned the captivity of Job...also the Lord gave Job twice as much as he had before.

JOB 42:10

Remember in the beginning, God referred to Job as perfect. Then He allowed all that he had to be demolished by Satan, breaking him down to his lowest point, having lost everything including his family and material possessions. Why? Because even though Job was living well, God saw greater for him. Therefore, He had to reduce him, put him back on the Potter's wheel, and behold who Job became in the end. That is God's plan for us too—to give us double for our trouble in the end. I, for one, am willing to endure as Job did and wait out the process as God has designed it. Are you? I can hardly wait to see the conclusion. How about you?

Hold on to the promises of God when He puts you on the Potter's wheel. It will not feel good, but it is for your good. Know that nothing happens in your life by chance; God has a purpose for everything, even when we do not understand (See Isaiah 55:8). Though God gives the enemy permission to disrupt our course every now and then, He always has a greater plan for the matter at hand. We must also know that He will always cause us to win in the end. The Word assures us that:

We are troubled on every side, yet not distressed; we are perplexed, but not in despair; Persecuted, but not forsaken; cast down, but not destroyed...

2 CORINTHIANS 4:8–9

> *...When the enemy shall come in like a flood, the Spirit of the Lord shall lift up a standard against him.*
>
> ISAIAH 59:19

We have to know that God will not have us go through for naught. Further, He will definitely vindicate us. It is simply a part of the process, and we just have to embrace it for what it is. Moreover, we should try to get used to it, as it is ongoing. We are His great work in progress—we are under spiritual construction at all times. Yes, He is going to continue to break us, shape us, mold us, and make us again and again and again. Then when He is finished with us, we will be made whole.

To Revisit the Potter's Wheel

It is one thing to have been placed on the Potter's wheel, to successfully walk through the process, and to be summoned to return to the Potter's wheel once again. Well, you might as well get used to it because there we will spend much of our time during that life-long sanctification process that I discussed earlier. The important thing to realize is that God is not punishing us, He is perfecting us. There are times that we will not respond to God unless we are under pressure, and thus He allows precarious situations to occur before us in different forms to shake us, causing a realization that there is yet more He needs to "work out" in us. Therefore, we ought to celebrate each of our Potter's wheel experiences knowing that God has our best interest at heart. Celebrate, yeah right!

> *And we know that all things work together for good to them that love God, to them who are the called according to his purpose.*
>
> ROMANS 8:28

Although we have this promise, the assurance that God will work all things out in our favor in the end, it is that which we must endure to the end that tends to seem unbearable at times.

One of my Potter's wheel experiences (of which I have had quite a few to date) spiritually crippled me for several months. As a Staff Sergeant in the U.S. Army, I was persecuted for not being able to follow through on a spontaneous mission—I was expected to leave my family with very little notice for an extended period of time. This occurrence blind-sided me, leaving me in a sort of wonder about what the Lord was trying to teach me. I later realized that God wanted to tutor me in how important it is to get past the eyes of men and what they think. At the time, I did not know that this life lesson would prepare me for the grand Potter's wheel visit that occurred during the separation from my husband. I must say that my separation brought about extreme hurt and made me feel embarrassed as well or maybe even more so than this particular trial (more details to be shared in chapter 9).

In the case of my persecution while in the military, I had to make a tough decision which was detrimental to my career. Though I was unjustly being mandated to go on an assignment that was presented to me, I was expected to follow the orders that were given. After seeking the Lord, I knew I had to obey Him and not man, and I had

to trust Him with the outcome that I was about to come face to face with. My results for refusing to deploy for that particular mission were extreme disciplinary actions. According to man's victory, I lost one of my stripes, my leadership position in my unit, and my annual review which had been previously written was changed to state completely derogatory information. Of course, I was devastated. But why did I have to go back to the Potter's wheel? It seems as though everything was being done wrong to me and not by me. What mars or blemishes did I have that I deserved this visit to the wheel?

Sometimes we are going along so fine, and we do not take the time to really check ourselves as God does. Even when those bad character traits are hidden behind the gifts, the talents, the smiles, God can see clearly those areas we need to confront. You see, God knows where He is going to take us and place us in the Kingdom. Therefore, He needs to work on us at ground level so that we do not embarrass Him when He sets us on top—releases us to the forefront. In my case, during this revisit to the Potter's wheel, God exposed my tendency to murmur and complain which was coupled with a little bit of unbelief. Sure I talked strongly about how I believed God in my situation, but when it was not wrapped in the victory package that I thought it should be, I fainted and grumbled despite how the Word addresses this conduct.

> *Do all things without murmuring and disputings: That ye may be blameless and harmless, the sons of God, without rebuke, in the midst*

of a crooked and perverse nation, among whom ye shine as lights in the world...

PHILIPPIANS 2:14–15

Here before me was a grand opportunity to be a witness as I walked through this; but I used much of it for my platform to declare that I was right, and they were wrong. Here was an opportunity to pray for the lost, that God would have mercy on them; but I found that I was more interested in God punishing them. To bring it home, I behaved this way primarily to cover up the embarrassment that I felt while going through this discreditable trial. It was hard for me to face those who knew how high I had climbed up the military ladder only to see that I had descended just a bit at the blink of an eye. God Himself had to crumble me down, reshape me, and put me back on His wheel to get rid of that mar of embarrassment which was coupled with murmuring, complaining, and doubt. Once He got me beyond the faces of people, He convinced me that man will never have the final say.

And Around...And Around

In the natural, once the potter has shaped, and reshaped the piece of art as necessary, having been satisfied that all blemishes are gone, he places it on the wheel. The piece goes around and around as it slightly glides through the hands of the potter. The potter gently guides this masterpiece with care. When God puts us back on His wheel, His intent is not just to have us crumble, but as with the potter, it is to turn our situations around. If we are honest with ourselves, we can recall His gentle touch as He directs us through every storm, bringing us out with the victory every time.

> *Fear thou not; for I am with thee: be not dismayed; for I am thy God: I will strengthen thee; yea, I will help thee; yea, I will uphold thee with the right hand of my righteousness.*
>
> ISAIAH 41:10

It seemed as though men prevailed against me when my rank was removed from my collar. However, God had a greater plan. Following that incident, I had made the decision to end my career in the military under the instructions of the Holy Ghost. When I did that, I was questioned and scrutinized by many, as I did not have a back up plan other than to just trust God. Following my decision, I had a miscarriage which I did not totally understand God's purpose for at the time. Because of my loss, my superior at the time authorized me to stay at home until I was completely discharged from the military. My expected date of discharge was scheduled for two months later. However, I was extended in order to undergo a medical board. To shorten the story, I will say that I exited the military one year later after being at home, in government quarters, with full military pay and benefits. Due to the findings at the medical board, I received severance pay in excess of $43,000 which was all tax free. Upon completion of an evaluation with the Veteran's Administration, I was granted a 40% disability rating which further resulted in full education benefits. I could go on, as the residual effects of it all are still pouring into my household, but I assume you get the revelation that God can and will turn it around. I say to you now, relax in your Potter's wheel moment. I promise you that God will not disappoint you when you dismount it without the slightest scratch or scar. Your patience will pay off in the end. I must say I waded through this trial as one would struggle wading through deep waters. It was not until God finished purifying me—my speech, my thoughts, my attitude—that He allowed me to realize the victory.

Chapter 6

The Refiner's Fire

Beloved, think it not strange concerning the fiery trial which is to try you, as though some strange thing happened unto you: But rejoice, inasmuch as ye are partakers of Christ's sufferings; that, when his glory shall be revealed, ye may be glad also with exceeding joy. If ye be reproached for the name of Christ, happy are ye; for the spirit of glory and of God resteth upon you: on their part he is evil spoken of, but on your part he is glorified.

1 Peter 4:12–14

Based on the verses of Scripture above, it may seem as though we are about to revisit the Potter's wheel yet again, but I assure you that we are not. Although the Refiner's fire brings about distress just as the Potter's wheel, the two does have individual functions. To understand the separation and correlation between each of these, we should define each naturally and spiritually.

> *However, the spiritual is not first, but the natural, and afterward the spiritual.*
>
> 1 CORINTHIANS 15:46 (NKJV)

Let me clarify by saying, in the natural the potter works out things that one is able to see on the outside. In view of the spiritual, such faults or mars are represented by bad attitudes, distasteful speech, gossiping and backbiting, willful disobedience in the presence of others, and any other visible character flaws. On the other hand, the refiner burns out those things that one cannot necessarily see but discerns something foreign is there. Likewise spiritually, these are hidden matters of the heart such as bitterness, anger, hatred, jealousy, envy, and the like.

Despite the distinction between them, in both the Potter's wheel and the Refiner's fire experiences, both are dealing with the process of sanctification. Having thoroughly discussed the Potter's wheel in chapter five, let us direct our focus toward our God being represented as the Refiner in this chapter. To do this we should first look closely at the meaning of the following words:

Webster's II New College Dictionary

Refine—To reduce to a pure state: purity; To remove by purifying; To free from course characteristics

Hebrew Dictionary

Refined—2212 zaqaq, *zaw-kak'*—to strain, extract, pour down, purge, purify, refine; 6884 tsaraph, tsaw-raf'—melt, purge away, try

As we can clearly see in each of these definitions, refining results in purification. The first definition suggests that reduction is required for something [someone] to reach the state of purity. Thus, we must decrease allowing God to mount the throne of our hearts, that He may be able to dethrone every thing that does not bring edification to Him.

> *He must increase, but I must decrease.*
>
> JOHN 3:30

Now let us turn our attention to the Hebrew meaning of "refined." We learn that it has classifications such as "strain, purge, and try" which all represent discomfort. Some trials that we may endure will cause us to wonder where God is and why He would permit such heartaches and pain, but we can be sure that He is watching nearby through it all. Fiery trials may come that would cause us to shut our spiritual eyes, disallowing us to see God fanning the flames all around us, but He is always by our side (See Hebrews 13:5).

> *Behold, I go forward, but he is not there; and backward, but I cannot perceive him: On the left hand, where he doth work, but I cannot*

behold him: he hideth himself on the right hand, that I cannot see him: But he knoweth the way that I take: when he hath tried me, I shall come forth as gold.

JOB 23:8–10

Go through the fire, we must, as God certainly has a plan for it every time. However, we should know that He is not standing by idly but rather with a sense of purpose for the end, to bring us forth as pure gold.

A Mother's Endurance

Fiery trials come in many different forms with all sorts of emotional triggers. For example, one's failing health, financial troubles, marital issues, hostile working environments, and parental struggles are just a few things that could prove to bring unpleasant disturbances in a person's life. To explain the Refiner's fire, I will use my personal battles and testimonies as a mother. And though I have three children, of which I have faced challenges with each of them, struggles with my son prove to be befitting for this discussion.

When I gave birth to Darius, I truly did not understand the concept of being a mother. My thinking was that buying him the cutest clothes and shoes would earn me the "Mother of the Year Award." How wrong I was. I enlisted in the Army about 6 months after he was born, leaving Darius in my mother's care during my training and while at my first two duty stations. Despite my warped view of motherhood, while I was away my mother did an excellent job of teaching Darius who his mother is. She, likewise, tried to create a relationship between Darius and his biological father, but all to no avail. From the time Darius was old enough to understand, he loved his father; but his scarce involvement in his life over the years brought about a lot of disappointments for Darius. This resulted in Darius' struggles with anger from the time he was a little boy. However, it was not until Darius was about 8 or 9 years old that we realized his anger would trigger behavior that was not normal or acceptable at school.

I had come to know the Lord just a few years before these episodes of anger began to manifest. Very early in salvation, we knew that the hand of the Lord was upon Darius' life. He also accepted Christ into his heart at the age of 9 and was filled with the Holy Ghost with the evidence of speaking in tongues by age 10. Then just as my husband and I started to grow in the things of God, we realized that the enemy was attacking us through our son. We had learned how to plead the blood of Jesus, pray prayers of faith, and everything else that was told to us to do; but we still continued to go through serious demonic activity with our son at home and at school.

It was during the time God blessed me to be at home awaiting the findings of that medical board discussed in an earlier chapter. God certainly knew I needed to be available for Darius at all times, as I was called to physically come down to his school 3–5 times a week for some sort of disturbance he had caused. His incidents ranged from throwing a desk or a ruler across the room to swinging a jump rope until it wrapped around another kid's neck. Imagine the exhaustion and emotional breakdown I experienced as I tried everything from discipline to love in all kinds of ways hoping to get to the core of my son's issues. I have since learned that Darius' behavior was as much about me as it was about him and vice versa.

Satan's ploy was to aggravate and distract me, as it was hard to focus on the things of God with so much going on with my child. There was a lot of embarrassment involved, and there were times that his reputation made it hard for us to advocate for him when I believed some things were handled inappropriately. In those cases, I found myself in disputes with administrators and faculty members endeavoring to see to it that Darius got the best education possible despite his anger which was beyond his control. A lot of times, I had to make great efforts to rid myself of bitterness toward those who blatantly attacked me due to frustrations that revolved around my son's issues. I found it hard, as we were often prejudged based on his disciplinary records or whatever information was passed along from one person to another. Oh the grief involved when a mother has to fight to preserve hope for her child. One who does not know any better might consider for a moment whether the fault lies within him or her, but this is not the case always. Scripture warns:

> *Yea, and all that will live godly in Christ shall suffer persecution...*
>
> 2 TIMOTHY 3:12

When one faces a fiery trial such as this or in any form, it is good to remember that your very walk with God will subject you to Satan's attempts to destroy you. So know that God is always strategizing to get some good out of whatever Satan does. As in my case, I did not know that I harbored such negative feelings toward those who were coming against me. I had even unconsciously allowed anger to creep into my heart toward my son for causing me such anguish. No way was God going to accept this, whether I acknowledged it or not. It was through these trials, the Refiner's fire that God allowed anger, resentment, and contention to rise up in me so that I could deal with it and ultimately dispel all of those impurities.

> *And he shall sit as a refiner and purifier of silver: and he shall purify...and purge them as gold and silver, that they may offer unto the Lord an offering in righteousness.*
>
> MALACHI 3:3

A Mother's Heart...A Mother's Pain

By happenstance, I am currently in the Refiner's fire with regard to my son, even as I have set a deadline to finish this book. One week away from completing this manuscript and all of hell has broken loose at my son's school. So not only am I going through the fire, but my son, who is now seventeen and in the 11th grade is accompanying me as God is heavily at work in his life right now as well. This time around, I do not have the option of throwing in the towel to wallow

in my sorrows. God has required me to be steadfast and to stay the course that He has set before me. Certainly my previous visits with the Refiner have equipped me for what we are dealing with now. We are about a week into this fiery trial, of which I will cover in some detail, and I have come to realize that God is in control and that my son and I have to position ourselves to ride this one out together.

It was the week of TBN's 2007 Spring Praise-A-Thon that my son was suspended from school for two days for disrespecting a substitute teacher. I was a little disgusted with him, and I informed him in front of the administrator that the punishment he received for that particular incident was just. So he came home with me and proceeded to do his assigned work. I felt compelled to watch a bit more of the Praise-A-Thon that day. Pastor Jamal Bryant was ministering the Word at the time. He began to speak words of confirmation to me that encouraged me about my son's future. I knew that we were in God's divine timing even though he was out of school for a negative action.

> *To every thing there is a season, and a time to every purpose under the heaven.*
>
> ECCLESIASTES 3:1

I made a pledge to sow a seed to seal the Word that had been spoken into our lives not even knowing that Darius was in agreement with what was being said. Though he was suspended from school, he was in the right place at the right time. Later that

night, Darius confided in me, telling me how God spoke to him through Pastor Jamal and how he wept all afternoon knowing that God was calling him to get in his rightful place. Immediately, I began to speak into my son's life and strategize with him the way in which we were going to realize his goal of going to Morehouse College in Atlanta, Georgia. Upon his return to school, Darius had a new attitude and a new outlook, but anger was still laying low in the recess of his heart.

Just three days after his return to school, Darius was in the hallway trying to calm down after an incident with another student. An unfamiliar teacher approached him and instructed him to go to class. Now he has an approved plan that affords him the opportunity to excuse himself from class and cool down if needed; however, he was not in the approved designated place. The teacher that came on the scene was insistent on Darius leaving the area right away, and he found himself in a quarrel with her. When another teacher came on the scene, security and all of the administrators were called. The results are as follow: Darius was accused of verbally and physically threatening to do bodily harm to the said teacher. He was expelled from school without a thorough investigation. When I arrived on the scene, Darius was upset, but not in any way insubordinate at the time. I had gotten there before the deputy who was called, but despite the fact that Darius was calm by then, I was told I needed to wait with him there and allow him to be arrested (of which I refused). The following day, a policeman was sent to my house to arrest Darius for intimidation of a public official, and my husband was threatened that he would be taken to jail as well for defending him. Back up police officers were called, as we would not allow them to take Darius without a warrant. In short, the Refiner's fire has been turned up just a bit higher than we knew we could stand. I believe I can relate to the testimony of Shadrach, Meshach, and Abednego. Let us look at their visit to the fiery furnace for a moment.

> *Then was Neb-u-chad-nez'-zar full of fury...therefore he spake, and commanded that they should heat the furnace one seven times more than it was wont to be heated. And he commanded the most mighty men that were in his arm to bind Sha'-drach, Me'-shach, and A-bed'-ne-go, and to cast them into the burning fiery furnace. Then these men were bound and were cast into the midst of the burning fiery furnace...the furnace was exceeding hot, the flame of the fire slew those men that took up Sha'-drach, Me'-shach, and A-bed'-ne-go...And these three...fell down bound into the midst of the burning fiery furnace. Then Neb-u-chad-nez'-zer the king was astonied, and rose up in haste, and spake, and said unto his counselors, Did not we cast three men bound into the midst of the fire?...He answered and said, lo, I see four men loose, walking in the midst of the fire, and they have no hurt; and the form of the fourth is like the Son of God. Then Neb-u-chad-nez'-zar...spake, and said...ye servants of the most high God, come forth, and come hither. Then [they] came forth...And the princes, governors, and captains, and the king's counselors, being gathered together, saw these men, upon whose bodies the fire had no power, nor was an hair of their head singed, neither were their coats changed, nor the smell of fire had passed on them.*
>
> DANIEL 3:19–28

The personnel in authority at Darius' school rose up against us just as those in the story of Daniel. After receiving the phone call about the incident, the Holy Spirit said to me that the matter at hand was "blown out of proportion," and it soon spiraled into a quest to persecute Darius. My calm demeanor was related to my faith that God can and will vindicate. However, the night following the incident, my son's tears were the evidence of how overwhelmed he was. He was shocked by the reality of what had taken place the day before and that morning when the police was trying to arrest him. There are always at least two sides to a story; however, as his mom, I heard Darius' heart (coupled with what I felt in my spirit) when he told me that things did not happen as it was reported. His hurt became my hurt, and I now fully understood that this is ultimately his Refiner's fire experience to behold. God was using this to purge him and to try him in order to prepare him for His service. As much as I was willing to envelop the heartache of this fiery trial for him, God encouraged me to step aside and allow Him to work on Darius. To date, we are still fighting to overturn some decisions that have been made, but through it all, I can see the Refiner at work in my son. It is as though I can hear an echo of the Lord speaking the following words to Darius in the hollow of his soul:

> *Behold, I have refined thee…I have chosen thee in the furnace of affliction.*
>
> ISAIAH 48:10

Victory, Victory Shall Be Mine...And Yours

In the midst of the onslaught of this trial, I notified several intercessors with the specifics, and every one of them immediately came in agreement with us regarding this matter. Though we still have a few uphill battles ahead of us, God has already begun to give us the victory in many ways. To date, the Sheriff department has called to inform us that according to the paperwork that was presented to them by the school, it is founded that Darius has not committed a crime. Thus, they are stepping out of the matter, no charges will be filed against my son, and he will not be sought out for questioning by them on this matter. To God be the glory!

I had to prepare Darius for the possibility of him not returning to school knowing the relationship between the administrators and me has been severed. This gave me an opportunity to minister to my son about God's plan and how it supersedes that of the enemy's. As the Scripture says:

> *But as for you, ye thought evil against me; but God meant it unto good...*
>
> GENESIS 50:20

Darius and I started to discuss how we would proceed from here moving toward his goal to go to college. We have come to learn that due to a special clause concerning him, he cannot be expelled without the opportunity to complete his credits. As a result, he is attending an afternoon program at another school which is designed to help him complete his classes. We are optimistic that he will finish the school year with the grades that he desires. Further, there are other community service opportunities that we are looking into for him to rebuild his reputation in preparation to apply for college. Even as God is working things out in the natural, He is yet at work in Darius' spirit as he spends his days in the comforts of our home, away from peer pressure, in the presence of God. Even as God has been overturning the plan of the enemy, I have reminded Darius that we cannot harbor any bad feelings towards those who are coming against us, but rather we have to continue to pray for them and keep our hearts pure. Whoa! I guess my Potter's wheel and Refiner's fire visits are paying off.

> *But I say unto you which hear, Love your enemies, do good to them which hate you, Bless them that curse you, and pray for them which despitefully use you.*
>
> LUKE 6:27–28

Although this testimony is very specific in nature, the outcome is universal. God always gives us "victory" in the end. We just cannot be deterred by the package that He wraps it in. So know that whatever fiery trial you may face or may be in the midst of right now will not overtake you.

> *Nay, in all these things we are more than conquerors through him that loved us.*
>
> ROMANS 8:37

Just read the remainder of the third chapter in the book of Daniel. Surely you will find that it was not enough that God kept the Hebrew boys in the midst of the flames; He accompanied them in the furnace. When they were released, their [our] God was exalted by the king, and the three were promoted. You, too, be encouraged that the Refiner's fire will not consume you. It is only preparing you for the great things that God has just for Y–O–U!

Part 3

When God Speaks: The Final Word

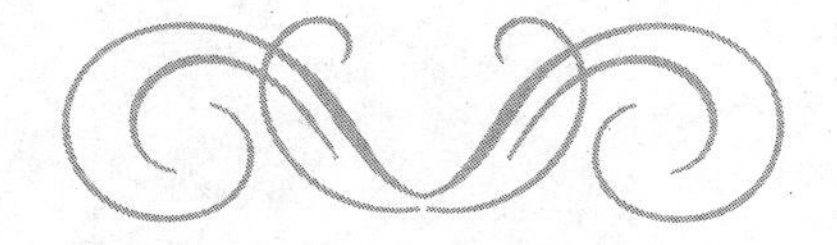

As we approach the conclusion of what the Lord is saying through *Worth the Wait* in this hour and season, we need to realize that this is it—His final Word. Either you get it or not. Either you believe it or not. Either you receive it or not. He has given to us divine instructions, and He does not plan to waver with regard to His conditions for us. When God speaks, that settles it. Consider the Scripture:

> *Jesus Christ the same yesterday, and to day, and for ever.*
>
> HEBREWS 13:8

There is a standard that God has set for the Church, and He does not plan to modify it. We must measure up to the example that is already in place—His Son. When we humble ourselves and strive to do so, He honors our effort. Further, through our obedience in putting Him first, we convince Him that we are ready to receive all that He has for us.

Chapters 7 and 8 further prepare and position us for the promises of God to be released unto us. Through these chapters we are encouraged to seek the Lord until we are certain that we are walking in true humility at which point we can fully return our hearts to Him, our First Love. These two chapters are followed up by chapter nine, the finale which offers an example—through my

personal testimony and a prophetic Word—of what God can do when we are in right standing with Him. Remember:

> *...no good thing will he withhold from them that walk uprightly.*
>
> PSALM 84:11B

Again, I want to remind you not to get hung up on the fact that I speak about my marriage, as God is a multi-faceted God. You can apply every lesson that I learned to your own situation. I merely use what I experienced to show the way in which God ministered to me, and the magnitude of what He had done for me in the end. Hopefully, as you get to the end of this journey, reading my testimony will help you to find hope that you can hold on to in your season of waiting as well, regardless of what you are waiting for.

Chapter 7

Discovery of True Humility

Humble yourselves in the sight of the Lord, and he shall lift you up.

James 4:10

Humble yourselves therefore under the mighty hand of God, that he may exalt you in due time.

1 Peter 5:6

Sure we are to set our sights high, aiming at the great things God has in store for us. However, we have to be careful not to practice self-exaltation which is a form of boasting or haughtiness. If we tout ourselves, then God has no need to shine His light of approval upon us. Further, we should heed the Scriptures that give us the following warnings:

> *Pride goeth before destruction, and a haughty spirit before a fall.*
>
> PROVERBS 16:18

For I say, through the grace given unto me, to every man that is among you, not to think of himself more highly than he ought to think; but to think soberly, according as God hath dealt to every man the measure of faith.

ROMANS 12:3

We must also understand that God has an appointed time to raise each of us up in the Kingdom, and He expects us to patiently await our turn. Though dwelling in a holding pattern may become aggravating, it is here that one might discover some of his or her personal character defects, namely false humility. Accordingly, it could be the case that lack of true humility is a hindrance to God's release of His promise(s) to you. I believe God has a wealth of blessings stored up for us, His children. All the same, I am convinced that true humility is the key to release it all. And the million dollar question is: What is true humility? Answer: The opposite of false humility.

False Humility vs. True Humility

To find where one fits into the scheme of things, one must first be able to differentiate between false and true humility. Let me start this section by first defining false humility. It is birthed out of pride which embodies a need to impress others. In some instances, one operating in this spirit searches for just the right thing to say or do in order to gain approval or praise from other people. There is another occasion when one intentionally downplays oneself to incite the praises of others as well. The latter is an extreme form of false humility, but it is real nonetheless. The confusing thing about false humility is that one wants to earn the endorsement of others but does not want it to be known that this is the case. Once desired results are realized, the individual goes to great lengths to ensure that any acknowledgement that is received is considered to be authentic and unprovoked which requires a constant balancing act. False humility could prove to be a full time task in that it takes a lot to ensure that one's mask is always in place.

Those who walk in false humility lack integrity. They do not keep their word, but rather conform to whatever demands they are presented with at a given moment to keep a steady flow of accolades. One must beware that the Word warns that this behavior will forfeit one's right to receive of God's goodness which contains the very thing that you are waiting for. Here is how the Lord sees it:

> *For he that wavereth is like a wave of the sea driven with the wind and tossed. For let not that man think that he shall receive anything from the Lord. A double minded man is unstable in all his ways.*
>
> JAMES 1:6B–8

Another thing to note about false humility is that it does not matter how much effort an individual expends to hide it; it still sticks out like a sore thumb. Though most people accommodate praise-seekers, they are usually very much aware of the individual's need to be recognized. Why? It is inevitable that the true intents of one's heart will tell the story on its own. Usually, one walking in false humility will do anything to protect his or her reputation without considering whether his or her actions will result in embarrassment. My take on this is that God only allows one to go so far pretending, and then He pulls the cover off—He brings about exposure. As the Scripture says:

> *For out of the abundance of the heart the mouth speaketh.*
>
> MATTHEW 12:34

True humility, on the other hand, is the product of a sincere heart. It is also walking in obedience to God while bringing glory to Him and not redirecting it to ourselves. Humility in its truest form exhibits selflessness, not self-seeking. Those who walk in true humility are meek and possess a gentle spirit. They know when to give up their right to be right so as to preserve peace, protect their witness, and display the true character of Christ at all times. Those who possess this trait are known for their ability to operate in silence and solace—knowing that God is always in control.

> *Let us draw near with a true heart in full assurance of faith...Let us hold fast the profession of our faith without wavering; for he is faithful...*
>
> HEBREWS 10:22–23

True humility gives one the assurance that spoken words are not always necessary, but rather recognizes that prayer is much more effective in any matter. Thus, those who walk in true humility heed the Word of God which says:

If my people, which are called by my name, shall hur
and pray, and seek my face, and turn from their wickec
I hear from heaven, and will forgive their sin, and will heal their lanu.

2 CHRONICLES 7:14

To summarize, true humility is the opposite of false humility which is described in depth above. However, the importance of this topic warrants a more specific definition. Hence, true humility is...

total submission to God.

to refrain from self-exaltation.

dying to one's flesh in obedience to God.

being able to give up one's right to be right.

acknowledging that we are all sinners saved by grace.

God's Got Your Number

God does not judge us by our facade or our good works alone. We should do everything as unto the Lord and not as unto man. Therefore, it is expressly important for our speech to parallel our walk with Christ—that what is in our hearts is depicted by our true character. There is a cliché that says, "Don't just talk the talk, walk the walk." I strongly believe God will reward us based upon how honest we are with ourselves and others as well as with Him. Further note that it may be possible to mask one's true identity and nature with people for a season, but God is always studying the contents of our heart. God's got our number.

> *...for man looketh on the outward appearance, but the Lord looketh on the heart.*
>
> 1 SAMUEL 16:7

Luke 15 records the intriguing story of the prodigal son. Allow me to expound on some its rich contents regarding humility, true and false in action.

> *...a certain man had two sons: And the younger of them said...Father, give me the portion of thy goods that falleth to me. And he divided unto them his living. And not many days after the younger son...took his journey into a far country, and there wasted his substance with riotous living. And when he had spent all...he began to be in want...And when he came to himself, he said...I will arise and go to my father, and will say unto him, Father, I have sinned against heaven, and before thee...And he arose, and came to his father...his father saw him, and had compassion...And the son said...I have sinned...and am no more worthy to be called thy son. But the father said to his servants, Bring forth the best robe, and put it on him; and put a ring on his hand, and shoes on his feet: And bring hither the fatted calf, and kill it; and let us eat, and be merry...Now his elder son was in the field...and asked what these things meant...And he said thy brother has come; and thy father hath killed the fatted calf, because he hath received him safe and sound. And he [the elder son] was angry, and would not go in: therefore came his father out, and intreated him. And he answering said to his father, Lo, these many years do I serve thee, neither transgressed I at any time thy commandment: and yet thou never gavest me a kid...But as soon as this thy son was come...*
>
> LUKE 15:11–14; 17–18; 20–30

Here we have one father and two sons with two distinct personalities. The prodigal son, if I may label him, is the "real" deal, representing true humility. He was forthright with speaking his heart's desire to his father. He was not afraid or ashamed to ask point blank for what he wanted up front. On the contrary, his elder brother can be considered a counterfeit, representing false humility. When his younger brother went away, he [the elder brother] worked for his father while secretly coveting his brother's boldness which gained him access to all that was in their father's house. The elder brother harbored bitterness in his heart while he pretended to be content in the state that he was in.

Upon the lost son's return home, after misusing all that his father had given him, he was honored all the more. Do not miss the moral in this story by wondering why he would be rewarded after committing such a sin against his father, and God for that matter. God looked beyond his faults and into his heart. There in the crevices He found an ounce or two of true humility which he allowed this son's father to see. In contrast, upon discovering that his father had received his son back with love and compassion, the elder brother accidentally allowed his mask to slip off. God exposed him for who he really was. When he learned that his younger brother was being honored, he immediately began to exalt himself by reminding his father of the good deeds he had done. He began to point the finger at his younger brother in judgment to justify his anger and jealousy. He painted a clear picture of false humility for us. Further, this story shows us that we may fool others and maybe even ourselves sometimes, but we have no chance of fooling God.

> *For the eyes of the Lord run to and fro throughout the whole earth, to shew himself strong in the behalf of them whose heart is perfect toward him...*
>
> 2 CHRONICLES 16:9

Not My Fault...Your Fault

As our marriage rapidly approached rock bottom, just before Keith and I separated, for weeks the tension mounted. We began to cast the blame on one another. We sought counseling from a couple we knew. We met them at a church we fellowshipped with periodically. It is as clear to me now as it was all those years ago. A meeting we had with our friends resulted in me feeling the need to stand up for myself. Apparently Keith had been having sidebar discussions with the husband which, today, I feel was totally misinterpreted as it was replayed to me. Nevertheless, at the time, I felt like the finger was being pointed at me, and my flesh did not respond to that very well. Before this event, I used to pride myself for keeping my cool. However, something on the inside of me wanted me to save face with this couple that I respected very much.

Our group discussion got pretty heated, and the husband drove Keith home, leaving me behind so that his wife could minister to me further. Instead, from what I can remember, I began to take this opportunity to point out all of Keith's wrongdoings. Now everything that I revealed was truth at the time, but my motive was totally wrong. My sole purpose for sharing all of those allegations was to reclaim my platform as the victim. The sad thing about this matter was that I was so concerned, at the time, about reclaiming my dignity that my marriage was pushed to second place of concern.

Before this incident, you could not have convinced me that another person's perception of me would cause me to react the way I did. Looking back on it now, everything that Keith shared about me which bothered him was, in essence, true. I was just so focused on his faults, having categorized it as worse than mine that I did not recognize my contribution to the turmoil we were experiencing in our marriage. I might have been honored that God wrote the following verses of Scripture especially for me if it were not for the fact that its purpose was to convict and to correct me. Thankfully, though, it accomplished its mission.

> *Judge not, that ye be not judged. For with what judgment ye judge, ye shall be judged: and what measure ye mete, it shall be measured again. And why beholdest thou the mote that is in thy brother's eye, but considerest not the beam that is in thine own eye?*
>
> MATTHEW 7:3–4

It took quite some time to grasp what God was trying to show me about myself, causing an even greater wedge between Keith and me. By the time he left our home, we did not speak to each other at all. As a matter of fact, there is a tattoo of the day he came home and

packed up his belongings, without saying one word to me, imprinted in my memory. Imagine the emptiness I felt not knowing where my husband would lay his head in the days to come.

Of course this is where grief was supposed to kick in, right? Well, it did not happen in that order for me. Rather than mourn my husband's absence, I began to talk about it out of my hurt. There was one person, my then pastor's wife, whom I confided in since the beginning stages of our marital trauma. I always knew her to be a person of confidentiality, and she was a listening ear through it all. Today, as I look back to recall some of the all–night conversations that carried and comforted me through it all, I realize that I worked very hard at shifting all the blame from myself to my husband. It was not that I wanted to scar or wound Keith; it was just easier not having to face myself. Therefore, I pretended to humbly await God's plan to manifest and His promise to be revealed in Keith's miraculous return home. As I lived the lie that it was all Keith and not me, I held up the blessings of the Lord. Thank God for not having a cut off time for me to get in the flow of what He wanted to do. To be perfectly honest, I do not even know when God got my attention and caused me to realize my lack of true humility. Who cares when it happened; I am just grateful that it did. I believe it is the perfect time for you, too, to pray the following Scripture to the Lord:

> *Search me, O God, and know my heart: try me, and know my thoughts...*
>
> PSALM 139:23

As I end this chapter, allow the Lord to minister to you about whether you are currently walking in false humility or true humility. If you found yourself in any part of this chapter, or even if you are not sure whether something that is just not right is tucked away, it is worth asking the Lord to reveal to you the true contents of your heart. Do not allow what you cannot even see to be a hindrance to you receiving what you desire to have from the Lord. Remember that it is humility in its truest form that will unlock the door to God's heart causing Him to exalt you in due season.

Chapter 8

Return to My First Love; My Second Love

The Lord hath appeared of old unto me, saying,
Yea, I have loved thee with an everlasting love:
therefore with lovingkindness have I drawn thee.
Jeremiah 31:3

When one comes to know the Lord by way of experiencing salvation—accepting Christ as Lord and Savior—he or she enters into a personal relationship with Him. Anyone who has had this experience can attest to the excitement one feels in the beginning stages of walking with the Lord. The phrase "tickled pink" comes to mind. Then something happens gradually. Somehow the zeal that was once known is no longer as strong as it was. In some cases, the witness begins to dissipate all together. A spirit of complacency takes over as one starts to plateau in this new—and at one time—exciting life. Eventually one is found in a backslidden condition.

To backslide in Christendom means to fall away from God so as to not live one's life as a Christian any longer. Normally when backsliding is discussed, it is in relation to someone committing a sin of which could be categorized as "a big sin." We, the people in the Christian circuit, tend to usurp the authority to decide which sins are unpardonable. Our reactions toward those who have fallen into various temptations tend to condemn our brethren in a way that God does not. Therefore, when one backslides it usually does not have anything to do with not being able to face God. It is the shame, the fear of how one will be perceived by people. How sad is that when the Bible encourages us in the following way:

> *Verily I say unto you, All sins shall be forgiven unto the sons of men, and blasphemies wherewith soever they shall blaspheme: But he that shall blaspheme against the Holy Ghost hath ever forgiveness, but is in danger of eternal damnation...*
>
> MARK 3:28–29

This passage enlightens us with the fact that God does not just push us away simply because we sin; we choose to back away from Him. It is as I spoke about in a previous chapter, that we set such a high standard for ourselves in salvation that we faint when we are not able to live up to it. That is not what God expects us to do, however. His desire is to see us get up, brush ourselves off, and keep moving in the things of God. Though He is not pleased with the sins we commit, He loves the sinner with an everlasting love as according to His Word.

As stated above, this is how backsliding is defined in Christendom. However, I would argue that there is a more subtle form of backsliding that not only involves the sin of commission, but the sin of omission as well. To explain my standpoint, let us look briefly at a few meanings of the root word, backslide:

> **Backslide**—to relapse, regress, or slip back; to drop to a lower level (Dictionary.com)

Here we see based upon these definitions, backsliding can occur without physically committing a sin. One can "not" do something and be found in a backslidden state. In relation to the meaning "drop to a lower level," one's regression in the ways of God—fasting, prayer, reading God's Word—can be classified as backsliding. Usually this form of backsliding occurs when someone or something slides in and threatens to take the place of God in our lives.

When Boy Meets Girl... When Christ Meets World

Let us take a moment to analyze the accounts of a teenaged boy and girl meeting each other. Sparks begin to fly, they feel butterflies in their stomach, and begin to daydream out of their classroom window. For days and weeks ahead they can hardly wait for the school bell to sound in between classes, taking the risk of getting caught by the tardy bell to see each other for just a moment, and back to class to repeat the cycle. Then the dismissal bell rings late in the afternoon, and that is another pinnacle in their day, as there is just one more opportunity to see each other before mounting the school bus to go to their perspective homes. If only the bus could do one less stop or go just a bit faster as their little hearts go pitter patter in anticipation for their next connection. They can hardly wait to get across the doorpost, settle in, and finish where they left off with a follow up phone call. Their silence is agreement with one another that I like you so much that it is just enough to sit here and listen to you breathe on the phone. Now the timeframe may vary on a case by case basis, but at some point the enthusiasm begins to fade. It is not that the thrill is totally gone, only the newness of the relationship. Sometimes other interests come into play. Whatever the case, there is a slipping back that often takes place. (Just a brief clip, but I am sure everyone can get the drift.)

This is the same exhilaration one feels in the embryo stages of salvation. It is as though one just can not get enough of God. A baby Christian eats, breathes, thinks, and speaks Jesus at all times—on a mission to tell the world about Him. Though the habits of prayer, fasting, and studying the Word of God has not yet been formed in this stage, there is an initial hunger that one experiences from the start. Behold how the Lord reacts to this yearning for Him:

> *Blessed are they which do hunger and thirst after righteousness: for they shall be filled.*
>
> MATTHEW 5:6

Though it is not intentional, just as with the boy and girl, we can easily reach a plateau in our relationship with God if we are not mindful to cultivate it. Regression usually takes place when we begin to slack in the amount of time we spend with the Lord. You see, when we enter into relationship with Him, our quest for more of Him is what converts our relationship into a love affair. In our pursuit to get closer to Him, we practice habits that are conducive to our growth in the connection we already have with Him. The more we do, the nearer He draws us to Himself.

Draw nigh to God, and he will draw nigh to you...

JAMES 4:8A

The Thrill Is Gone

It is puzzling to think how we go through roller coaster moments in our relationship with God. One day we are on the mountaintop, and the next we are down in the valley. Yesterday we were on fire for God, and today we are struggling to last ten minutes in prayer. What happens to all that stamina from the early days? Where does the excitement go? My answer to that is: "Nowhere!" It is still there waiting to resurface. It is hiding in the background, behind whatever new pleasure that you are consumed by. Though it may not be your intention to push God out of the spotlight in your life, welcoming something or someone in to share it with Him causes Him to step aside. As we discussed in great detail in chapter four, He refuses to share His glory.

We must be mindful of God's promise to never leave or forsake us (See Hebrews 13:5). However, we have to be willing to extend the same courtesy to Him. We fail to do so when we do not exclusively reserve a space for Him in our hearts. In consequence, we find ourselves committing spiritual adultery, in a love affair with whomever or whatever is enjoying the front seat in our lives at the moment. The tricky part is that we often have trouble recognizing that we are in this place. Much thought toward this is discussed in chapter four, so I will be careful not to be repetitive. However, I will say that once we recognize and then acknowledge our poor judgment, God awaits our full return back to Him with outstretched arms. As a matter of fact, He will meet us and aid us to give us what we need in our return to Him.

> *And I will give them an heart to know me, that I am the LORD: and they shall be my people, and I will be their God: for they shall return unto me with their whole heart.*
>
> JEREMIAH 24:7

Upon God's return to His rightful place in our lives, and our unwavering return to Him, He brings with Him divine order and structure that we never knew.

Love Lessons...Instructor: The Master Himself

To put God first, allowing His love to permeate our lives without measure will prove to be rewarding in every thing and for everyone

of importance to us—our spouse, our children, our career, our ministry. When all else becomes secondary to God in our lives, He can teach us through our relationship with Him how to cherish all else that matters. Otherwise, when we offend God by placing Him second, causing Him to stand on the sidelines, we have to rely on our own wisdom to care for those people and things that mean the most to us. In contrast, when God is first, we can be certain that He will lead, guide, and direct us with regard to all which concerns us. He will reveal to us in prayer and through His Word exactly how to entreat the treasures that He entrusts to us. When we are in right standing with Him, He gives us all we need upon request.

> *If any of you lack wisdom, let him ask of God, that giveth to all men liberally, and upbraideth not; and it shall be given him.*
>
> JAMES 1:5

> *How sweet are thy words unto my taste! Yea, sweeter than honey to my mouth. Through thy precepts I get understanding: therefore I hate every false way. Thy word is a lamp unto my feet, and a light unto my path.*
>
> PSALM 119:103–105

Before closing this chapter, I will revisit my coming into the knowledge that I loved my husband more than I loved God. Upon recognizing this and repenting, I did not automatically fall madly in love with the Lord at that point. It was through a process—through consistent prayer, praise, worship, the Word—over a period of time that I fell in love with God all over again. In retrospect, I was able to love Keith on a level that I never knew to be possible. I had read and studied agape love, but in all honesty it was not in my heart at the time. How could it be if my love for God was tainted? However, upon my return to God, my First Love; I developed an authentic, unconditional love for my husband, my second love. I am sure he does not mind taking that position next to the Lord. There is no timeframe I can elaborate on. One day, I just knew. Today, I remain—in love with my Lord, in love with my husband in that divine order as it should be.

As I look back on some of the things that I endured during the time that Keith and I were separated, of which I will discuss in detail in the next chapter, I am amazed. I know today, that it was only through the love of God that I could love Keith the way I did through my pain. When I slid back into God's loving arms, I was able to ask Him to teach me how to love my husband beyond his faults. I used to ask God when we were separated to preserve the love that I had for Keith and not allow me to waver based on what I faced with him. Today I am still standing and can declare that God, through his infinite love and wisdom, did all that I asked Him to do. You, too, can return to your First Love and experience the same fulfillment in whatever or with whomever you allow to assume the position next to God. I promise you that God Almighty will not disappoint you if you would put Him first today.

Chapter 9

A Divine Reversal

**For with God nothing shall be impossible...And he said,
The things which are impossible with men
are possible with God.**

Luke 1:37; 18:27

Sometimes life tends to take us by surprise, bringing us unexpected woes. Even so, we are to remember that we serve a God who sees and knows all things. Further, He is not idol, but rather is responsive to the cares and the needs of His people. In such complex times, we are left with one choice—to trust God and take Him at His Word:

> *For the word of God is quick, and powerful, and sharper than any twoedged sword, piercing even to the dividing asunder of soul and spirit, and of the joints and marrow, and is a discerner of the thoughts and intents of the heart.*
>
> HEBREWS 4:12

When life deals us a hand of cards that we do not quite know how to play, we must rely on God. When it seems like there are no answers to the questions we have regarding situations we come face to face with, we must still ask God. When the problems that we have appear to be beyond finding solutions, we must still petition God. When we are faced with the impossible, we must continue to trust God. His Word encourages us to:

> *Trust ye in the Lord for ever: for in the Lord JE-HO'-VAH is everlasting strength.*
>
> ISAIAH 26:4

> *Cast thy burden upon the Lord, and he shall sustain thee: he shall never suffer the righteous to be moved.*
>
> PSALM 55:22

As you are nearing the end of this journey, you have been taught through prophetic insight and revelation how to prepare and position yourself for your long awaited breakthrough. It would not make much sense to come all this way and not believe you are able to attain what God has for you. I know your vision, your circumstances, your mountain—whatever it may be—is huge and may even seem insurmountable to you. What can I say to that? So what! Almighty God, as the Bible declares:

> *...is able to do exceeding abundantly above all that we ask or think, according to the power that worketh in us.*
>
> EPHESIANS 3:20

Now there are those of you that have lost hope, feeling like the enemy has taken his best shot and succeeded. You may feel like you cannot recover, that your situation offers little or no hope. You might have totally given up, thrown in the towel, and is ready to accept defeat. Well, the Lord sent me to tell you and to serve notice on the devil that He is getting ready to do *A Divine Reversal* for you. He has commissioned me to write this book so that you will know that absolutely nothing is too hard for Him.

Though chapter nine is the finale, its contents actually drive the entire message of *Worth the Wait* and offer an example, through my testimony, that God can do the impossible. Despite the fact that I introduced excerpts of my testimony throughout the book, prepare yourself, as I am going to candidly and openly reveal it all—everything that God brought me through. To demonstrate the awesomeness of God, I find that it is necessary to disclose the severity of my circumstances and how God was able to overturn them. It is my sincere desire that everyone who is privy to read the accounts of what God did for me will find hope in whatever state they are in. My primary purpose in this assignment is to impart, into each of you, faith that will move mountains.

> *For verily I say unto you, That whosoever shall say unto this mountain, Be thou removed, and be thou cast into the sea; and shall not doubt in his heart, but shall believe that those things which he saith shall come to pass; he shall have whatsoever he saith.*
>
> MARK 11:23

Surely God did not have me to endure all that—communication classes, the Potter's wheel, the Refiner's fire, love lessons, etc.—for naught. Therefore, it is my belief that *Worth the Wait* is not just for a select group of people. Because the message is universal in nature, I believe it is global and that the world should have access to it. Having accepted this mandate from the Lord, I plan to see it through to completion and mass production. Also, by the end of this journey I hope to convince you that what God has for you is for you, and you will find when you receive it that it will have been *Worth the Wait.* And now for the moment you have all been waiting for—my personal testimony:

Honeymoon's Over

Having already shared with you the details of how Keith and I came to know the Lord in chapter one, I will fast forward to the turbulence we began to experience when Keith started getting cravings for drugs once again—the very thing that God had delivered him from. It was about two years or so after we were saved, so this was a strange occurrence to us. He shared it with me, and we prayed together attempting to overcome these temptations. Now during this time he ministered, once a week at the military prison on the base where we lived. He was rooted in the things of God and could pray fire down from heaven. To say the least, as far as we knew he had a sure foundation in Christ.

Though we sought counsel and prayer from our leaders, the temptation eventually overtook Keith, and he went out and got high one evening. You know how the enemy puts it, "Just go do it once so that you can get it out of your system," he told Keith. Well, he did try it as the devil suggested, but that was not the end of the story. This was devastating for both of us, as we had been doing so well. We walked together in the Lord, ministering and serving at our church. After being counseled by our leaders, Keith repented and made the decision to go on with God. That was a relief, as neither of us was prepared to go back to where we came from.

In the days ahead, the cravings grew stronger and stronger. Keith succumbed to them while still reaching out for help to overcome this demon that was now overpowering him. Now that the door was opened to the enemy, he came all the way in and brought some friends with him, one specifically by the name of rebellion. By the beginning of 2003, his struggles worsened and his relapses were more and more frequent. We consulted our pastors, and they prayed with us and even sought out help for Keith, all to no avail. Eventually, Keith threw in the towel. He did not want to fight it anymore.

Throwing in the Towel

In March, 2003 we were set to have our housewarming and were getting the final preparations in order. The night before our celebration, we were each doing our last minute shopping. I had spoken with Keith that evening, and we were set to meet up at home together. He never showed. By this time, guilt was a big factor and caused him to reject my phone calls whenever he was out getting high. He came home just hours before all of our church family arrived. No one knew what had taken place the night before, but the Lord allowed our pastor to pray from his spirit for us, and I thought for sure Keith was getting a breakthrough.

Much to my dismay, by May of that same year, Keith decided not to return to church. Again, guilt was unbearable for him. At the time, he was the head deacon at our church, and he had just been acknowledged as an aspiring minister about six months earlier. He was such a faithful person in the Kingdom of God that he would never do God halfway — he was not a pretender. He would rather stay away than fake salvation. In everything Keith did, he maintained an all or nothing attitude which in this case caused him to turn and walk away from God so as not to straddle the fence with God.

Though it was progressive, it was almost as if it happened overnight. Once he completely stopped going to church, it seemed as though all of hell invaded our home and our marriage. Up to this point, our children did not know what was going on, as I shielded them from the truth of it all. Because Keith worked a job that kept unusual hours, it was not strange for him to be gone at odd times. I just endured it, hoping that God would deliver and we could move on. Unfortunately, it did not play out that way. Keith wanted to give up drugging so badly that he was willing to do almost anything.

Knowing his love for his children, he thought that telling them to hold him accountable would be enough to make him quit. Well, it was not.

Walked Away...Pushed Away

Now that the children knew, this made it more difficult for me. Every time he was gone, they relied on me for answers since we could not make contact with Keith. In my distress, I got it in my head that something had to be done for the children's sake. The friction had increased between Keith and me to the point that he had started talking about leaving. At some point, I began to prepare myself for a separation. Then I went beyond preparing and started to pursue it. Somehow the enemy had convinced me that things would be better with him gone, even though I still wanted my husband. I took it upon myself to file for a separation, making it clear to the representative that I did not want a divorce, and that I wanted my husband to return eventually.

In July, 2003 I told Keith about the paperwork that I had filed, and that we needed to arrange for him to be served. That sure did not go off as smoothly as I expected. That instance sowed a seed of rejection into Keith. We argued and fussed, and in my ignorance at the time I could not believe his reaction to all of it. I thought he should have just accepted it since he was planning to leave anyway. Instead, he felt like I was pushing him out of his home and his family. Though I was not, I was unable to convince Keith at the time that this was not my intent. I merely thought it would be easier if he were gone completely, for a little while, so that the children did not have to always wonder where he was and what he was doing when he was outside of our presence.

A Rough Ride

Me, in my arrogance and ignorance at the time, thought more highly of myself than I should have. In my mind, I thought he might only last a week or so away from me. Can anyone believe that I esteemed myself higher than God, who was still wooing Keith to come back to Him? Well, 2 weeks turned into 2 months, 2 months turned into 2 years, and I was still believing and waiting for Him to bring my husband back home. Unfortunately, my wait was not being stretched out over a bed of roses. Neither was it like tip-toeing through the tulips. I cannot say that I knew when I embarked upon this boat, called waiting, exactly how rough the ride ahead of me would be.

Because of Keith's anger toward me, there were no limits to what the enemy was going to use him to do to afflict me. During our separation, I was told, "I am in a relationship with somebody else; I have moved on; I am never coming back." I experienced watching a woman pick my husband up in front of our church once he brought our children to me. I have witnessed him moving in with a woman. I have called his cell phone, only to get the voice recording of a woman adjoining their names together instead of ours. I lived through Keith telling me that another woman was pregnant, and he planned to move on with his life with her. I endured him being arrested and asking me to contact the other woman for him and cussing me out when I refused. From the mouth of the man who promised to cherish me for the rest of my life, I heard foul words spoken to me that are too vulgar to grace this text. I could tell you more, but that is enough for you to understand the magnitude of what I needed the Lord to do for me, and for you to understand that He can do what you need Him to do for you. Commercial break: I can hear enquiring minds asking the question, "Why would you put up with all that?" My answer to your question is this, "Because the Lord told me to." You, too, have to become so familiar with the voice of God that you know exactly what He is speaking to you about your situation—what you are waiting on Him to do for you.

To Know Your Assignment

When Keith left our home, I told the Lord that I want my husband to return, and if He would keep me, I would wait. The Lord's response to me was, "Daughter, if you wait, I will make it worth your while." Now, I did not know all of what I would endure as spelled out above. God had to constantly remind me that it was not Keith whom I was dealing with, but Satan using him in attempts to destroy our marriage. So, I could not focus on the "stuff" that I had to endure but rather the promise that was made. I could not dwell on the criticism of man about why I would accept what was happening before and to me. I had to set and keep my eyes fixed on the prize.

My philosophy is this: If I am a woman of God and a woman of faith, then my prayers will be answered eventually. So having invested years of prayer in this man, I knew that God would eventually deliver him, set him free, and use him mightily. Therefore, I will wait because after all that I have prayed, I refuse to walk away and watch somebody else reap the benefits of what God would do for me. I had no choice but to stay the course.

God gave me a mandate about one year into the separation that I would tell the story in a book. He told me that the book would be entitled *Worth the Wait.* God was so specific that He told me the book would have nine chapters. He gave me the names of each of those chapters at the same time, and you are reading the fruit of it all, as not one thing changed from the time he gave it all to me about three years ago. I had no choice but to trust God and wait, as one cannot tell a story about something one has not experienced. How could I have written *Worth the Wait* if I had not waited to see what God would do or how He would move for me? I could not. Glory to God, my Keeper!

While enduring all of what I described above, I was a full time student in an extremely challenging accounting program at the University of Washington, Tacoma. It was so hard to keep focus that I sought out the psychologist who did not understand why I wanted my husband back. Each time I talked to her, I unveiled all of my hurts just to feel slightly relieved enough to make it through another day. I would then end each session by telling her something like "I still trust

God, and I am still going to wait, and that Keith would be home in time to be seated in the audience at my graduation." Now having been steadfast and unmovable with regard to what the Lord promised me in the beginning of this separation for over a year and a half, I was starting to get weary. I needed some assurance that the Lord was going to move for me. I felt a shift in our situation, as Keith had become quite pleasant with me. Suddenly, he was much more attentive and responsive when I called him. Somehow I got the courage to talk about reconciliation with him.

By Any Means Necessary... When God Has a Plan

The perfect day to have "the big discussion" would be on Keith's birthday, March 4, 2005 since he had accepted my invitation to take him out to dinner. Unfortunately, dinner ended in tears of sorrow rather than tears of joy. Before I could begin to talk about my desires to reconcile with him, Keith informed me that a female was pregnant for him. Ironically, that is not what shook me because I had prepared myself early on for that possibility which would hurt, but was not a criterion for me to give up on him and God's promise for our marriage. The devastating thing in the conversation was that Keith told me he wanted to move on with this woman, whoever she was. That night I left him broken and confused, as he thought that the news of a woman being pregnant would sway me from waiting any longer. He was caught by surprise as I told him that I knew God did not have me wait all this time for nothing, and I was still not going to give up but rather continue waiting until God brings him back home.

Though I spoke such strong words, I was weakened by the discouragement I felt from learning that after all this time, I still had to wait a while longer and with the thought of my husband wanting to have a new life with someone other than me. God hurriedly reminded me that it was not my husband that I was dealing with but rather a seed of the enemy. Even so, I was crushed. That Friday night I got myself home and crawled into my bed; clothes, shoes, and all. This assignment from the devil was designed to take me out. The prayers of the Saints carried me through that particular weekend, as I could not even pray for myself. I made it from Friday to Monday and had to return to school; but I knew I could not go any further without a breakthrough.

That morning the Lord spoke to me, instructing me to fast nine days for my husband. Before I left my home for school, I got on my living room floor on my face before God. I told Him that I would lot leave my house until I get a breakthrough. I began to agonize and travail in prayer from the depth of my belly. I started praying what I knew to pray until the Holy Ghost took over my tongue. Out of my mouth without thought came these words with such force, "God, I need you to do *A Divine Reversal!*" Those words shook me so that I stopped praying for a moment. When I realized those words were not my own, I continued on as the Holy Spirit led. When I got up from the floor, I knew that hell's plan for our marriage was interrupted.

Within weeks, Keith was stopped by the police and arrested. He did not call and tell me, but the Holy Ghost revealed it to me. He was shocked to see me in the court room at his arraignment. Even so, the Lord told me not to intervene and that He would be released in due time. The woman who was said to be pregnant at the time was with Keith when He got arrested, but the police let her go. Keith gave all of his money and other possessions to her and expected her to bail him out immediately, but she left him stranded in jail (or should I say the Holy Ghost did). Though he had never even mentioned this woman's name to me, in desperation he told me he needed me to contact her. When I refused, he went ballistic, but I stood my ground that though I loved him, I would not degrade myself in that way. I made contact with the couple he lived with at the time, and they began to make efforts to get him out. God held him captive for four days. By the end of those four days, he had called and apologized to me and wanted me to come and visit him in jail. He said we needed to talk, and I knew that God was changing his heart. However, he was released before he could have a visit, and he decided not to return home at that time. I knew the Lord was at work, so I was okay with it for then. Keith discovered some things about the young lady spoken of earlier and to make a long story short, God did *A Divine Reversal*. It was still March, 2005 and this event renewed my faith to continue holding on to the Word of the Lord regarding my marriage.

Renewed Faith to Hold On

From that point, Keith was different toward me even though he was not ready to come home. Understand that all this time, there was no intimacy between the two of us, as I was not going to play the role of a girlfriend with my husband. I had to totally wait on God to restore every part of our marriage. I continued to give as according to the Word of God, sowing seeds of faith from the very beginning. Though in the natural I could not afford to give, in my spirit I knew I had to give. I must share that God honored every seed of sacrifice and was faithful to keep me. I did not get a sugar daddy to help pay the bills. I relied on God who supernaturally paid every single one of them on time—mortgage, auto loan, utilities, credit card, groceries, etc. I did not sneak late night phone calls while my children were asleep. I relied on our Everlasting Father who wrapped me in the cradle of His arms every single night. In short, He kept me completely.

Though God kept me, I must share how the enemy subtly sent the temptation for me to deviate from the plan of God. Beforehand, God hid me in a glass bottle for the first year which made it easy for me to hold on. It was as though He shielded me from men for a season. If I were being flirted with or pursued, I missed it. However, one day the Lord opened that bottle and let me out. It was during the summer of 2004 that I had started a new job, as I was going to lose two forms of my income while not attending school during that time. I was hired for a part time, temporary position working at a seasonal military camp where officers were being trained. Within days of being on the job, the enemy sent his ambassadors on assignment to trip and to trap me.

There were two men in particular that appeared to take interest in me despite my wedding rings that I never removed. The ironic thing is that it actually felt good to be noticed at the time. Though I did not want a relationship with these men, the enemy began to toil with my thoughts of my need for companionship which I did not struggle with before this time. I can remember thinking ridiculous thoughts like, "I can go out. I am not planning to do anything. I can just be a friend. It will be fun. Friendship won't destroy my witness." Now I knew that these thoughts were straight from the pit of hell, and I hurriedly dispelled them. Within three weeks, God removed me from that job and took care of every financial need as He did before. You see, when the enemy's plan to use our trials (in my case, being separated from my husband) to destroy us fails, he attempts to use us to annihilate ourselves. His goal is to cause us to miss out on the promise that God has waiting to fulfill for us. In my case, God exposed the enemy's ploy, renewed my faith and my mind, and He kept me in spite of Satan's plan.

When I Really Believed... When You Really Believe

At some point I became content in the state I was in. Somehow my faith was restored when I did not even realize that it had been. I just knew God was going to do what He said, and I would just take it as it came and in whatever package. I knew something was different between Keith and me once God moved the last mountain that I talked about. He came on our family trips, and still no intimacy, but we enjoyed being around one another with our children. He began to spend quite a bit of time at our home even though he did not move back in. I knew God was up to something, but I did not want to get my hopes up by setting anymore time limits. I just enjoyed the moment we were in and continued waiting on God.

The children and I left to spend seven weeks in South Carolina with our family, but Keith could not go because of his status with the courts at the time. However, he met up with us in New York for a weekend to attend his sister's wedding. We had a wonderful time, and he showed me off to his family as his wife. Most of the extended family members were not aware of our separation because we live so far away. When the festivities were over, he left to go back to Washington, and the children and I drove back to South Carolina for a few more days. We returned home to Washington on Wednesday, August 31, 2005. On Saturday, September 3, 2005 –3 days later—I got a phone call early in the morning. The voice on the other end had the following to say:

Lonnie, I've been out here long enough,
and it's time for me to come home.
Can you come and get me? I love you!

I went into shock for about a week or so, as the promise of the Lord had chased me down and overtook me by surprise. Hallelujah!

Now even after Keith returned home, went through drug rehabilitation, and made the decision to return to school to attain a degree in computer networking, the enemy yet raised his hand against our household. Another young lady gave birth to a baby boy, partially named him after Keith, and then announced that the baby was his. He was served with papers to appear in paternity court for DNA testing. Again, I began to pray, God summoned me to yet another fast, and one of the things I wrote down was to have my husband's name cleared. I did not concern myself with it; I just left it with the Lord and continued to remain focused, as Keith had now become a full time student as well, and I was getting ready to graduate. Come to think of it, I need to call and tell that psychologist that Keith did make it home in time to cheer me on from the stands as I walked across the stage at the Tacoma Dome having received my Bachelor of Arts degree in Accounting in June of 2006. Further, in July of 2006 we received papers in the mail that the courts excluded Keith as the father of the child, clearing his name as I had fasted for. Once again—*A Divine Reversal.*

Excuse me while I take a praise break...You should take one too because in the Name of Jesus, I prophesy unto you that *A Divine Reversal* is about to hit your house as well. The Bible declares that:

> *...even God, who quickeneth the dead...calleth those things which be not as though they were.*
>
> ROMANS 4:17B

Prophetic Word for Every Reader

> *The Word of the Lord to you this day is that He is going to restore to you the years that the locusts, the cankerworm, the palmerworm, and the caterpillar have eaten up. You will never be the same. Thus saith the Lord, even the message of Worth the Wait has fallen on good ground this day, and because you have received My Word, not just in your ear but in your heart and your spirit, you will never be the same. Know this day that eye has not seen nor ear heard, the things that I have prepared for you. As you keep your heart pure toward Me as according to the instructions given throughout this book and in my Word, I will overturn the plan of the enemy for you over and over again. You shall walk in victory, so just hold on because it is going to be Worth the Wait!*

When God speaks, the Word is final and all we need to respond with is Amen! So be it!

P.S. Even on this very day April 27, 2007, as I bring this book to a close on my 36th birthday, I have to share with you one very

momentous event as evidence. This morning the same man whom the enemy drove away from his family, swearing never to return again, served me breakfast in bed with a rose and a card that said, *"I Love You, Your Husband, Keith E. Perry."* Dear Reader, I told you it was *Worth the Wait!* Also, I am neither embarrassed by, nor do I regret any part of what I endured. As a matter of fact, by way of it all, I have been ***Pushed Into Destiny!*** Stay tuned...

Continuation

I certainly hope that you enjoyed the journey with me through *Worth the Wait.* It certainly was a pleasure writing it, as I have been ministered to through the revelations that God gave me to share with each of you. Surely this was a divine assignment, and I am so blessed that God chose me to do it. As you read this book, I hope you reached the end with rejuvenated faith, knowing that God has neither forgotten you nor the promise He made to you. He is Alpha and Omega, the Beginning and the End. Therefore, He already knows what is before you.

> *For I know the thoughts that I think toward you, saith the Lord, thoughts of peace, and not of evil, to give you an expected end.*
>
> JEREMIAH 29:11

Worth the Wait is a seed of encouragement that I am sowing into the Kingdom of God to remind the Body of Christ that God is able. I use much of my personal testimony relating to my marriage, my military experience, and motherhood throughout the book merely as an example of what the Master is capable of doing if we take Him at His Word. I declare that as He moved for me, He will move for you in whatever way you need Him to.

And they overcame him by the blood of the Lamb, and by the word of their testimony; and they loved not their lives unto the death.

REVELATIONS 12:11

Then Peter opened his mouth, and said, Of a truth I perceive that God is no respecter of persons.

ACTS 10:34

Since conclusion suggests that the story has ended, I feel it is befitting to call this part of the book Continuation instead. There is so much more that I expect God to do, and so should you. Therefore, I guess you get to hear from me again in the near future about what more God is doing in our lives and what He is able to do in your life as well. Specifically, the ninth chapter is prophetic in nature in that I am trusting God for the completion of what He has started.

Being confident of this very thing, that He which hath begun a good work in you will perform it until the day of Jesus Christ.

PHILIPPIANS 1:6

So shall my word be that goeth forth out of my mouth: it shall not return unto me void, but it shall accomplish that which I please, and it shall prosper in the thing whereto I sent it.

ISAIAH 55:11

You, too, must continue to believe God for your long-awaited promise. Do not give up, give out, nor give in. You are closer than you think to your miracle. And I promise you that it is *Worth the Wait!*

So many things we need God to do
Give an answer, solve a problem, or just see us through
Whatever the need, He knows just how to move—
It's Worth the Wait

Whether it's a bill you don't know how you'll pay
Or you couldn't afford to go out for lunch today
Be encouraged—It's Worth the Wait

Maybe it's a rebellious kid that won't mind
Or your teenaged girl you can't seem to find
Hold on!—It's Worth the Wait

Could it be that job you don't enjoy anymore?
Or the boss whom you less than adore
Maintain your dignity—It's Worth the Wait

You're frustrated with your accomplishments
And your loved ones give you very little compliments
But that's okay—It's Worth the Wait

You thought you'd be married by this age
Instead you're still alone and secretly enraged
Don't faint Dear One—It's Worth the Wait

You thought you married Mr. Right
Rather you experience day to day fights
Endure—It's Worth the Wait

Or could it be that Mr. Right walked out on you
You're devastated, and the children too
Trust God—It's Worth the Wait

God has shown you a bit of His plan
It's so great you need a few helping hands
Don't get discouraged—It's Worth the Wait

No one understands the calling on your life
Your attempts to convince others often end in strife
Holdfast—It's Worth the Wait

Whatever you are believing God for
Know that He alone is the open door
Hold on to the promise of God, whatever it my be
When you walk in it you will declare it was—Worth the Wait!

Y.C. Perry, Original

Look What the Lord Has Done!

Keith & Yolanda Perry

The Perry Family

Keith, Darius

Kyra, Yolanda, Kadazia

What therefore God hath joined together,
let not man put asunder.
Mark 10:9

All photos were taken on 05/25/07 by G. Tobias Milloy
www.photosbytobias.com

About the Author

Prophetess Yolanda Chevette Perry led the Women's Ministry at Living His Word Evangelistic Ministries for five years. Through this experience, she gained the confidence she needed to give birth to a vision that God gave her for a women's outreach ministry. Today she is the founder and president of Sister 2 Sister International Ministries based in Spanaway, Washington. Sister 2 Sister International was founded on January 10, 2007. Prophetess Perry is on the ministerial staff and is active in the women's ministry at Divine Revelation Ministries in Tacoma, Washington under the leadership of Pastor Paul L. Tabron, Sr. She ministers each month at the Washington Correction Center for Women (Prison Ministry), and she has witnessed hundreds of souls saved and lives transformed in this ministry over the last 8 years. She also served 11 years with the U. S. Army, and after she honorably ended her military service, became a full time student at Pierce College. She graduated from Pierce College, having received honors such as Dean's List and President's List recognition during her tenure and also received the 2003 Business Student of the Year Award for her outstanding performance in Economics. In June of 2006, she received her Bachelor of Arts degree in Business Administration/Accounting from the University of Washington, Tacoma. Prophetess Perry is a hidden treasure that God is now ready to share with the Body of Christ. She is known for her charismatic and demonstrative delivery of the Word of God. God is calling her "out of the shadows and into the light" for such a time as this. It is this work that has now given her the new title of "accomplished author."

Yolanda Perry was born and raised in Beaufort, South Carolina to Mr. Benjamin Allen, Jr. and Mrs. Shirley Allen. She is married to Keith Eric Perry of Mt. Vernon, New York. Mothering her three treasured children is listed among her greatest accomplishments: A son, Darius JaVar and two daughters, Kadazia KeSahn and Kyra Elise Perry.

Contact Information

Yolanda C. Perry

P.O. Box 4523

Spanaway, WA 98387

(253) 875-7718

Email address:

yolanda.perry@sister2sisterinternational.org